An Offering of Rice

stories by
Mavis Hara

ISBN-10 0-910043-76-0

ISBN-13 978-0-910043-76-2

This is issue #90 (Fall 2006) of *Bamboo Ridge, Journal of Hawai'i Literature and Arts* (ISSN 0733-0308).

Published by Bamboo Ridge Press

Printed in the United States of America

Indexed in the American Humanities Index

Bamboo Ridge Press is a member of the Council of Literary Magazines and Presses (CLMP).

Cover: "Indigo Lotus Suite, #4" by Noe Tanigawa. Oil and encaustic on lutrador, 1996. Title page: from "Summer 1999" installation by Noe Tanigawa. Charcoal on lutrador, 1999.
Section breaks: "an offering of rice" by Noe Tanigawa. Charcoal on paper, 2007.
Design: Rowen Tabusa

Bamboo Ridge Press is a nonprofit, tax-exempt corporation formed in 1978 to foster the appreciation, understanding, and creation of literary, visual, or performing arts by, for, or about Hawai'i's people. This project was supported in part by grants from the National Endowment for the Arts (NEA) and the State Foundation on Culture and the Arts (SFCA), celebrating forty years of culture and the arts in Hawai'i. The SFCA is funded by appropriations from the Hawai'i State Legislature and by grants from the NEA.

Bamboo Ridge is published twice a year. For subscription information, back issues, or a catalog, please contact:

Bamboo Ridge Press
P.O. Box 61781
Honolulu, HI 96839-1781
(808) 626-1481
brinfo@bambooridge.com
www.bambooridge.com

5 4 3 2 1   07 08 09 10 11

SEP 1 7 2014

For my daughter

Thank you to editors Eric Chock and Darrell Lum, and copy editors Normie Salvador and Milton Kimura for their patience. Thank you to Noe Tanigawa for allowing me to use her beautiful images and to Rowen Tabusa for his photography and book design. Thank you to members of Study Group for their extremely valuable criticism and suggestions. And thank you to staff members Wing Tek Lum, Joy Kobayashi-Cintrón, and Xander Cintrón-Chai because they make everything possible.

Table of Contents

Reverie in the Morning

We are swaddled together
in the morning's first light.
You are just one month old,
and I cradle you contentedly
in my arms,
burrowing back
into the cushions
of my mother's old koa couch.
Your empty bottle lies near us,
just after your burp,
you manage a sloppy smile.
You stare intently at my face
and I stare at yours,
and you surprise me
as you begin to sing.
A liquid song,
no consonants,
maybe the same song
you sang only weeks ago
when you were still inside,
in the dark.
Is it the sound of the water that surrounded you
being stirred by
the beating of your birth mother's heart?

Maybe you used to sing this song
to her then,
when her protective water filled your lungs,
and your feet kneaded her bladder,
and your body was cradled securely
by her bones.
Perhaps it is your song of thanksgiving
for her blood,
which supplied all your needs.

It may be a mistake you have made
about who I am
that inspires you to sing to me,
but I shamelessly smile my acceptance,
and you fill your lungs
with more bright morning air
and sing again, a wild sound,
which surprises you
as it vibrates in the light.

The Tanuki's Song 1920

"Sho sho Shojoji	"Sho sho Shojo temple
Shojoji no niwa wa	Shojo temple's garden
Tsu tsu tsuki yo ni	On nights when the moon is full
Minna dete koi koi koi	Come out, come out, everyone
Oira no tomodacha	All of our friends
Pom poko po no pom	Drumming, pom poko po no pom
Makeruna, makeruna	Don't lose, don't lose
Osho san ni makeruna	Don't lose to the priest
Koi koi koi koi koi koi koi	Come, come, come, come, come, come
Minna dete koi koi koi"	Everyone, come out."

It was Sunday, Mikiji sat in his wicker chair next to the window. Above him hung his *papale*, straw hats. The door to his smoking cabinet was within easy reach of his right hand, his four sons were at baseball practice, the afternoon sunshine was thick and warm, the house, wonderfully quiet. He settled back into his chair and nestled into the patchwork cushions. Behind him in the kitchen, his oldest daughter had just finished cooking the rice for their dinner. The rich smell from the rice pot floating through the house encircled him gently. Eating white rice with every meal was something he had become accustomed to in Hawai'i. He closed his eyes and rubbed his hands though the short gray stubble atop his head. His six children were all alive and healthy. He was able to send a small amount of money back to Japan each month. Outside the back door, the lean-to he had built and used as a hothouse was filled with orchids. He sighed. Life in Hawai'i was good, he had been incredibly lucky.

"Kill me too! *Watashi mo korose!*" A woman's scream cut into Mikiji like the knife-sharp edges of sugar cane leaves.

"What's the matter with you? If you kill yourself, do you think I can ever take this child and go back to my family? Don't think only of yourself. Kill me too. Go ahead. Go ahead!"

The sound came from the direction of Arai's house. Mikiji stood up and shivered, suddenly cold. He bolted out of his house and ran toward Arai's. The ground was muddy from the afternoon's rain. His feet squished tiny brown waves as they pounded over the boards laid on the dirt of the alleyways between the houses.

"Mama . . ." the long, thin scream of a child. He ran faster, wanted to be there and yet was afraid of what he might see. He passed wooden houses like his with rusted *totan* roofs. Between the houses, plants potted in coffee cans stood on makeshift shelves of boards. There were no large green lawns, no tall trees, just plants high off the ground in coffee cans, their owners refusing to let them put roots down into the soil. The cooking smells drifting slowly out of kitchen windows eddied around him as he ran and disappeared into the agitated wake behind him.

"*Oi*, Arai, *yamete yo*." A large group of people was gathered, fifteen or twenty neighbors trampling down the tall California grass that grew wild around the unpainted brown house. He saw two of his own sons, on the way home from baseball, among the crowd of people.

"*Oi*, Arai, *dete kite*." Some of the men were calling. "Stop it, Arai, come out." There was no answer from the darkness inside the house.

"*Doo shita*, what happened?" he panted toward one of the men dressed in a blue and white cotton *yukata* over a white undershirt.

"Arai's gone crazy again." The man snorted. "Drinking, he's got a razor. Going to kill himself." The man spat on the mud.

"What about his wife and son?" Mikiji asked. The man frowned and lifted his chin in the direction of the doorway.

"Inside."

"Ha, ha, ha . . . *koi, koi, koi*, come, come come." It was Arai's voice. "*Makeruna, makeruna* . . ." They could hear him singing. "*Mina dete koi* . . . ha . . . ha . . . ha . . ." They could hear his laugh echoing inside the house.

"Maybe he'll kill them and then kill himself," one of the women said as she circled around to the open back door. She held one hand over her mouth until she was behind the tin can on the back porch that held the scraps of discarded food that the farmers came to collect to cook into slop for their pigs.

From her shelter behind the large can, she yelled out, "Come out, Setsuko, bring the child and come out." She jumped back quickly as a green sake bottle was thrown from inside the house. It crashed against the tin slop can then skidded across the porch spilling sake onto the dark wooden boards.

The crowd gasped and became silent. Mikiji felt as though cold sake had been poured over him. He remembered the days twenty years ago on the Hilo plantation. He and Arai had been young workers together there. He suddenly realized Arai had said the same things on the plantation. Mikiji looked at the tall grass that was creeping toward the house from the overgrown yard. Mikiji remembered the song Arai had been singing then.

The sugar cane on the Hilo plantation looked like tall grass, like the wild grass that grew back home in Japan. But in Japan the farmers like Mikiji and his brothers towered over the daikon and cabbages, the millet and rice that grew in their fields. They were taller than the wild grass that grew in the uncultivated meadows. Here in Hawai'i, the cane loomed over Mikiji as he worked in the day. He could hear the leaves rustle above him as he and the other field workers slept in their shacks at night. He had stopped feeling like a farmer. Working in the cane made him feel like one of the animals that lived in the fields and meadows back in Japan, like a rabbit hopping through dry stalks, or a fox disappearing quietly behind rustling leaves, or . . . .

"*Minna dete koi, koi, koi.*"

The moon shone through the tassels of the sugar cane making it look like the picture of the *susuki* grass on a set of *hanafuda* cards. Someone was outside their plantation shack singing a children's song.

"*Oi, sempai.*" It was Arai. Arai greeted Mikiji with respect as a younger classmate greets an upperclassman at the same school. Arai was drunk and smiling. There was an innocent sweetness in Arai's smile.

"Arai! You should be sleeping. They will wake us up early tomorrow morning and make us work all day again in the fields." He frowned at Arai. "We must sleep as much as we can so we can stay strong." He scolded Arai as it was proper for a *sempai* to instruct a younger classmate.

"I'm not going to school tomorrow, *sempai.*" Arai smiled brimming with mischief. "Tomorrow, I go to see them in the meadows. I'll go and call to them." Arai turned drunkenly and danced, crouching and squatting, shaking his shoulders and wiggling his head from side to side. "*Oira no tomodacha pom poko po no pom.*" He threw out his belly and made a drumming motion on it.

"*Baka!* Stop your stupid singing!" Mikiji said. He would have shouted it but there were other men sleeping in the shack. "Come back inside now, Arai! This is no time to sing children's songs under the moon," he whispered furiously instead.

Arai smiled innocently up at Mikiji. He pulled a long thin towel from inside his cotton *yukata* robe and twirled it between his hands. He then wrapped it over the top of his head and tied the ends together under his nose. He lifted one foot, then the other and pivoted in an unsteady circle.

"You're drunk!" Mikiji sputtered. "Stop this *bakarashii* singing now!" He felt his anger rising and welcomed it like warm water. He let it splash over himself like water thrown on the body to wash the sweat of fear away.

"Makeruna, makeruna.
Osho san ni makeruna.
Koi, koi, koi, koi koi koi
Minna dete koi koi koi."

Arai sang and laughed until his sides shook, then ran off like a small animal into the stalks of cane. Mikiji shivered. He remembered the crazy people in his village in Japan. They always acted as if they had been bewitched by foxes or *tanuki*. Here in Hawai'i, the work was too hard. Mikiji was hungry all the time. The *luna* on horseback herded them like animals. It was no wonder Arai began acting strangely. The *luna* shouted orders and carried whips. The Japanese contract workers went to work in the dark. They worked all day in the fields and came back home in the dark. They slept in shacks, shoulder to shoulder on the wooden floors. Arai had been restless since they arrived here. He had not been sleeping with the rest of them at night. And now he was running around out there in the dark. Mikiji walked around outside the hut. He peered off into the cane. He could not see Arai and did not know if he wanted to. Finally, he went back into the shack and lay down to try to sleep.

He closed his eyes but Arai's song would not leave him. He remembered the pictures of the *tanuki* in their schoolbooks. He remembered the hot summer nights, all the shoji doors open, the smell of incense burning to keep away the flies that would bite you and make you scratch until you bled. He remembered lying on the futon safe under the mosquito net, drifting away into sleep and his mother singing.

"Sho, sho Shojoji
Shojoji no niwa wa."

His mother sewing, touching the blue-black thread to the camellia oil in her hair. He remembered the indigo-dyed fabric handsewn into a carpenter's bag. He blinked back tears, shook off the thin blanket and fumbled open the wicker suitcase at the foot of his sleeping mat. He dug through clothes to find his carpenter's bag, unwound the dark blue cords that held it closed and took out a rectangular chisel with a razor-sharp blade. Arai was only singing a children's song. He would be back in the morning. Mikiji put the carpenter's bag beneath his blanket. He lay down and closed his eyes but gripped the chisel tightly in his right hand. The scent of his mother's hair oil clinging to the dark cotton bag enfolded him and carried him into sleep.

The *luna* on horseback reminded Mikiji of the samurai. You never looked at them if they passed you in the field. In Japan, it was a samurai's right to draw his long sword and cut through a farmer's body. The samurai would write a letter of apology to the farmer's family and leave a few gold coins. No one would question him. That is how it was done. The *luna* was riding though the cane field toward them.

"Be quiet, Arai!" Mikiji hissed. Arai had been back at the shack in the morning and joined them as their work gang left for the day. Arai had been smiling all morning as if he had found an *oni*'s treasure and eaten a pile of rice balls all night under the moon. The *luna* pulled his horse to a stop beside the row of cane the men were hoeing.

"You falla, *hana hana*," he barked at them as he saw Arai leaning against his hoe and smiling. The other men in their gang melted back into the cane. They knew this *luna* well. He was smaller than the others and he carried a leather whip. The other men knew his bad temper and the only sound they dared to make was the chunk, chunk, chunk of their hoes biting rhythmically into the ground.

"*Makeruna, makeruna*," Arai sang as he waddled up to the *luna*'s horse. He smiled up at the *luna*, and then, as if he were doing something perfectly natural, he took off his clothes. The others in the work gang murmured as they stopped hoeing and gathered to watch.

"*Osho san ni makeruna,*
Koi, koi koi, koi koi koi koi,"
Arai had surely gone crazy, but they all knew the words he was singing.

"Don't lose to the priest.
Come out, everybody.
All of our friends.
With our drumming
We can drown out the priest's chanting
We can win."

Arai danced in a circle, lifting one leg high then the other. Then he crouched grotesquely and made a drumming motion on what he seemed to think was an enormous imaginary stomach.

The *luna* didn't understand Japanese but he knew he was being challenged by the vulgar fool's gestures. The overseer shouted a curse and reached for his whip. Mikiji watched in terror as Arai, smiling drunkenly, danced on. The *luna* brought the whip cracking down in a glancing blow on Arai's naked side.

"Arai, *yamete!*" Mikiji began screaming. "Stop it! Stop it! Arai!" The work gang huddled together. Arai flinched as the whip raked him but stood up again and lurched once more into his crazy dance.

"*Oira no tomodacha* . . . our friends . . . " he sang. The whip cracked again. Mikiji felt his knees shaking, but Arai was from his hometown, his younger classmate in school, and Mikiji, unable to watch any longer, lunged forward to pull Arai away.

"*Makeruna!*" Arai screamed and ran in a crouching charge toward the *luna*'s horse. The animal whinnied and reared up. Its hooves flailing outward caught Arai in the head and shoulders and he went down. Mikiji watched in horror as the *luna* gained control of the horse and raised his whip over Arai's motionless body.

Just like the samurai, Mikiji thought, trembling, but suddenly he realized, THE *LUNA* HAS NO SWORD. Mikiji jumped forward to protect Arai's body from the blow and felt the sting of the whip as it wrapped around his hands. Then he pulled. He could feel the rough hair on the horse's heaving side. The *luna*'s leather boots were kicking at the horse, at Mikiji's face. The horse's snorting began to merge with the *luna*'s shouted curses and Mikiji's own breathing. He held on to the whip though he felt as though his arms were being pulled off. Suddenly, he heard someone yell in Japanese.

"*Gambare!* Fight!" The power of the words shot through him. He grasped more tightly at the narrow bands of leather cutting into his hands. He pulled. The *luna* screamed as he fell forward. Instantly, the whole gang of Japanese men was surging around him. Someone else yelled, "*Gambare!*" then, "*Make-runa* . . . don't lose!" and many rough hands reached up and pulled the *luna* out of the saddle and onto the ground. The wind blew the white tassels of the cane and whistled through the giant leaves. Mikiji looked up and, for a moment, it seemed as though the struggling men were *tanuki* and foxes framed by stalks of *susuki*, pampas grass, in a bewitched scene on a gigantic *hanafuda* card. The *luna* without a horse became a frightened rabbit who threw back his head and squealed. Someone found a piece of rope and the *luna* who had been a rabbit was tied like a chicken. The air was filled with loud laughing and shouting. Kyushu curses, rough country language echoed through the long grassy stalks.

"Bury him."

"Dig faster!" They all used their picks and hoes. The blades churned the ground until the *luna* was buried up to his neck and looked like a *daikon* root floating in a *furo* bath of earth.

"Arai?" someone called. "Is he dead?"

"Over here. He's alive!" They picked Arai up and carried him back to camp leaving the *luna* like a giant turnip planted in the *tanuki*'s new garden.

Now Mikiji edged close to the unpainted steps of the old house.

"Arai. *Oi,* Arai-kun. It's me, Mikiji," he called. He could see shards of the broken sake bottle glistening like little knives on the rotting, cracked wood of the porch. The others murmured as they realized he was going to walk inside the house. Mikiji stepped across the threshold into the cool darkness and sweet sake smell inside the house.

"What are you doing, Arai-kun? Everyone is making a big fuss outside about all the yelling in this house." As his eyes became accustomed to the dim interior, Mikiji could see Setsuko and the boy Teruo huddled in a corner. She was tiny, even for a Japanese woman, but strong as bamboo. Another woman would have run back to Japan after realizing what kind of man she had been given to in an arranged marriage. But Setsuko held her head up and accepted an impossible situation. Other women in the camp called her Okusan, an honorary title for a wealthy married woman, to award her admiration. He turned toward the smell of sake and his heart began to race as he saw Arai crouched in a corner. The sun glinted off the rectangular blade of the razor in Arai's right hand. Mikiji walked slowly forward, until he stood between Arai and the woman and child.

He turned his head to whisper to Setsuko, "Are you all right?" He could see her nod and pull the child close to her. "*Dete ike,* get out." he whispered urgently.

"It's only because he's been drinking ever since we got the letter from Japan about his mother," Setsuko whispered, her face tear streaked. "Nowadays he's been working every day and . . . "

"Go now," Mikiji interrupted, "go call the judo sensei to come and help."

At first she hesitated, not wanting to leave, but at last she tugged the child up and began edging toward the door. "*Ki wo tsukete*, be careful, Mikiji-san." The small boy was frightened and tried to cling to her, and they lurched clumsily together and backed into the family's Buddhist altar. Setsuko turned to steady the little plates of food and the vase of fresh flowers.

"Leave it, take the child and go!" Mikiji whispered to her again. Setsuko scooped the small child up into her arms and backed out toward the doorway. Mikiji's feet tingled as he hoped she would not step on the glass scattered across the porch.

"What are you doing, Arai?" he said softly. He could see the stubble of Arai's beard, black and white hairs poking though the skin like coarse fur. Arai was standing with his feet spread wide. His cotton *yukata* was open below the waist. He had pulled his *yukata* skirt up above his thighs and was crouched like an animal, his breath rasping heavily in his throat. Arai was edging away from him, backing into what Mikiji, who had never been inside before, knew must be Arai's corner of the house. Setsuko's side included the kitchen, the sewing box and *tansu,* and the altar. The floor was smooth and polished on that side, the plates and bowls on the shelves in the kitchen neatly stacked. Arai was backing into a dark corner filled with sake bottles and *hanafuda* cards. He had set his sake bottles in a line like offerings at a shrine. Mikiji followed Arai into the dark. The glint of metal was a powerful reminder to be cautious.

Arai was sitting in a corner. Mikiji could hear his labored breathing.

"Arai-kun. What are you doing?" Mikiji called. "Why do you need the razor? "

"Okāsan," Arai called forlornly. "Okāsan is dead. She did not wait for me," Arai whined. "I promised her I would come back with so much money," he went on. "Okāsan! I promised her, but every month, the cards." He began throwing handfuls of cards in the air. "Not my fault, the cards." Arai began to sob in alcohol-saturated grief, his tears falling on the *hanafuda* cards scattered like maple leaves across the floor.

Mikiji was frightened. He remembered that years before, Arai had charged at the *luna*'s horse. Mikiji had been young and strong then. Now he felt his knees ache. His body shook with each of his thudding heartbeats. He was becoming an old man. He wished that the judo sensei would arrive at the door, he wished that he could have someone to help him. But he and Arai were alone in the house. He heard the clink of metal. Arai had put the razor down. Mikiji moved forward across the room, and then reached out to grasp the razor. Arai, though drunk, was quicker, reaching for the razor's handle as fast as a centipede. Mikiji grabbed for Arai's wrist and caught it in his fist. Arai bolted up with the strength of a wild animal. Mikiji struggled to hang on to the hand that held the razor as Arai pulled him along.

"Arai . . . stop . . . stop." Mikiji was thrown suddenly to the floor in the kitchen. Arai thrashed about wildly, knocking over Setsuko's carefully stored food supplies. Something heavy landed on top of Mikiji and he struggled to stand up. He dared not loosen his hold on Arai's hand. He heard the noise of the razor penetrating fabric, but was surprised that he felt no pain. Suddenly, he felt a torrent of tiny grains pelting his face and chest. Arai had sunk his razor into a 100-pound bag of white rice.

Arai sobbed like a child at Mikiji whose hand was still locked on his wrist. Mikiji could smell the stench of stale sake on Arai's breath. Mikiji had been horrified at the flow of the white grains. Rice in their Japanese village had meant the difference between life and death. The sons helped their fathers in the fields until they were married. Men and women worked together all of their lives. Elderly grandparents and stillborn infants were buried in small hillocks in the middle of ricefields, where with each rainstorm, they could return to the earth and be reborn as round rice grains.

"Arai-kun, it's me, Mikiji! Stop crying!" Mikiji screamed, but Arai's eyes were tearful. "Arai-kun . . . "

"*Ka-chan no tokoro ni kaeritai!*" Arai shouted in a child's petulant voice. "I want to go home to Mama's house!" He tugged at his wrist, trying to free it from Mikiji's grasp.

From his position on the floor under the rice bag, Mikiji watched as Arai squinted and began staring intently into the shadows in the kitchen. Suddenly in the middle of his sobbing, Arai began to laugh. Mikiji felt the hairs on the back of his neck rise. He struggled to sit up to look over the rice bag to make sure there was nothing in the darkness. Mikiji shuddered. Arai, sensing Mikiji's weakness suddenly pulled his wrist free.

Razor in hand, Arai scampered away toward the far corner of the house. Mikiji could see Arai stop and stare at the veins in his left arm. Arai had strong, hard muscles that had been built from his years of work as a stevedore on the docks. The veins in his arm stood out as clearly as the ropes that were used to tie large bales of cargo. Mikiji was horrified as Arai swiftly swept the razor across his veins in a clean glinting arc. Mikiji watched as blood flowed down Arai's arm in a red rivulet. The torrent of blood ebbed and flowed like a priest's chanting across a temple yard, like Arai's luck with *hanafuda* cards, like the lucid and clear moments in Arai's mind. Though Mikiji was not the one who was hurt, he felt the room spin. He swallowed hard. He moved his foot and felt it slip. He watched Arai in horror as more blood began to flow. Arai began to rock unsteadily. Mikiji heard screaming, but Arai's mouth was clamped into a tight line. Mikiji suddenly realized that it was his own voice he was hearing. The screaming gave him strength. His head cleared. He pushed the rice bag off his chest and leaped across the room. He grabbed Arai's wrist with one hand and with the other snatched the razor away. He hurled it out of the house over the doorsill. He heard the clink of metal and glass as it slid across the porch.

Arai reached for Mikiji's shoulder and Mikiji tensed to fight off an attack. He was surprised as he felt Arai's gentle touch and looked into his clear eyes. "*Sempai . . .*" Arai whispered.

"The doctor! Where is the doctor?" Mikiji screamed out the door.

"*Oi* . . . Mikiji . . . . Are you all right?" someone called from the outside.

"Send a doctor," Mikiji yelled back as he put his arms around Arai to catch him as he slumped to the floor. Setsuko rushed in through the door dragging with her the three women who had been trying to hold her back. The midwife with her black bag and the judo sensei pushed into the house together.

"You hurt, Mikiji?" asked the sensei.

"Arai, Arai . . . . He's bleeding!" Mikiji said, gingerly extending Arai's arm to show them. The judo sensei's hands expertly probed for pressure points where he pressed down hard to stop the bright red flow of blood. The midwife quickly covered Arai's wounds with white bandages. Setsuko pushed Mikiji aside and cradled her husband's shoulders and head.

Mikiji sat back heavily on his buttocks. His legs had begun to tremble and he needed to feel the comfort of the floor beneath him. He could no longer see Arai, who was surrounded by a crowd of people. Mikiji's hands began trembling too, and he put them down on the floor beside his thighs. He felt a prickling sensation. He was surrounded by grains of white rice. He picked them up one by one and laid them gently in his lap. In their village, rice was planted, tended, harvested, dried, and threshed by hand. Each grain was precious. The family did not grow rice for food. Rice was grown to pay taxes. The family collected the few grains that were left after the samurai seized the government's share. These were hoarded and mixed with flakes of pressed barley.

"*Sempai* . . ." Arai was calling softly. Mikiji struggled to his feet unsteadily, scooping the grains of rice into his palm. "*Sempai* . . ." Arai said again softly. "*Aho da na* . . . I am a fool," he sighed. Arai's eyes were filling with tears.

"Arai-kun," Mikiji said, and put down the grains and took Arai's arm in both his hands as he knelt next to him on the floor. "*Gambare,* Arai," he said. "You remember, the plantation, where we buried the *luna*? Remember what you were singing that day? You sang, '*Makeruna,* don't lose.'"

The judo sensei, Setsuko, and several of the neighbor men lifted Arai onto a wooden door, which they used as a makeshift stretcher. The vegetable man had volunteered his truck, and they were on their way to the hospital, several blocks away. The neighborhood women were in the house, busily cleaning up the spilled rice. They worked on their hands and knees, picking up each grain, refusing to overlook even one. The women made cushions out of children's old clothes, they collected and brewed tea out of *obako* weeds, they saved scraps of food to feed the pigs, they used jelly jars for glasses, they refused to waste anything. Mikiji had often wondered why Setsuko stayed with Arai, and realized suddenly that in the same way that a woman could never waste rice, Setsuko felt she could never waste a husband.

Mikiji watched as Setsuko, the sensei, and the neighbors loaded Arai onto the flatbed. Arai clung to his wife's hand.

"Otōsan, can Teruo go home with us tonight?" Mikiji looked up at his eldest son, Toshi, and his younger brother who stood with their arms around Teruo's shoulders. Mikiji saw that his sons were growing tall and thin like stalks of sugar cane. Mikiji's sons, who had their grandmother's eyes, would never have to face a *luna*'s whip or a samurai's sword. He felt his soul unfurl like a bolt of silk washed in a river's cool waters. Arai's son, Teruo, small-boned and supple as bamboo, was not sobbing or crying, in spite of what had just happened. Mikiji could see that the boy had inherited much from his mother.

The evening wind whispered through the bamboo grove next to Arai's house making the slender stalks wave slightly in the wind. The stalks and leaves made the same whispering sound as a paddy full of rice plants. Mikiji remembered that there was a pot full of white rice on the stove at his house. "Let's all go home and eat," he said.

An Offering of Rice 1935

Tatsue wanted to stay downstairs and listen to the new Rudy Vallee song on her mother's radio, but Okāsan was sick with asthma again and it was not easy for her to climb the stairs. Tatsue sighed as she uncovered the pot of freshly cooked rice and pressed the sticky grains into tiny brass dishes. The grains held together like a white moon. Okāsan taught her that rice offered to the ancestors and the gods should be smoothed and round, not triangular like the *musubi* humans ate because there were no corners in heaven. In Japan, they said everything in heaven was a circle.

Tatsue carried the offering dishes upstairs and put one plate of rice in front of the Shinto shrine and one in front of the larger Buddhist shrine. She lit three thin sticks of black sandalwood incense and planted the sticks upright in a bowl of gray ashes. Then she sat back on the silk cushion and whispered the name of the Buddha, "Namu Amida Butsu."

Tatsue did not sit long. She left the rice at the altar until the incense burned away and added itself to the ashes in the bowl. While she was upstairs, she collected the family's laundry—a rice bag full from the room that her four brothers shared, another from the room she shared with her sister Kei, and the last bag from Otōsan and Okāsan's room. She carried all the bags down the stairs and left them next to the galvanized tin washtub beside the copper furo.

"Tatsue, *hayaku yasai wo arainasai*," Okāsan called, and Tatsue hurried upstairs to collect the dishes of cooled rice from the altars then back downstairs to the kitchen to help wash the vegetables for dinner. When she got there, the two littlest children, Masao and Kei, were waiting.

"I want to eat the *mamai-san* rice," Masao said.

Tatsue wished that just this one time she could eat the cold rice in the brass dishes but she gave Masao one of the servings and six-year-old Kei the other. The two children smiled happily as they chewed on their prizes. Okāsan was already at the sink slitting the belly of the fat mullet she had bought from the fish peddler that afternoon. Tatsue avoided looking at the red intestines and the gills that sent blood swirling into the sink.

After dinner, Tatsue finished washing the dishes, and then went back to the laundry room where Otōsan had heated the water in the copper furo. Behind her in the back room, she could hear someone crying. Someone was always crying. This time, it was the little one, Masao. He was tired of following

Kei around the house and wanted to go outside with his older brothers. And he didn't want to wear Kei's old dresses anymore.

"I like pants," he cried. He was three now and knew the difference.

"*Yakamashii!*" shouted Otōsan and Masao sat down on the floor reduced to soft whimpering. He had seen Otōsan hit the older boys with the belt before.

Tatsue scooped hot water from the *furo* into one of the tin laundry tubs, then set the wooden washboard inside. She wanted some new clothes too. How she envied Nī-san, her older brother. He worked at Fair Department Store and always got to buy new things then acted so high-nosed when he wore them.

She filled the second tub with cold rinse water and opened the rice bags and began to sort the clothes. She pulled out a sweat-streaked shirt. It was Yoshio's now. She remembered washing it when it belonged to her big brother Nī-san. He and Otōsan had not spoken to each other since the night Otōsan told him to leave school and work full-time.

"*Shikata ga nai.* Can't help it. You have to work," Otōsan had said.

"One more year I going finish!" Nī-san had argued. "One more year I can work anyplace I like. I can make big money. Why you cannot wait one year and let me graduate?"

"*Naze yuu koto kikan no?*" Otōsan yelled at him. "What kind of son are you? Men have to work." The old man had stood firm as iron in the end, so Nī-san did as he was told and handed over his paycheck every week. But he spent all the money Otōsan gave back to him to buy the latest clothes.

"Hardhead. Make Big Face every time," Tatsue whispered to herself. "Think he too good for us now."

Tatsue dunked and scrubbed. As she worked, she could hear her mother coughing in the back room. Okāsan could never do all of this work by herself, and the boys would never set foot into the laundry to help. "Woman's work," they called it. But tomorrow Tatsue could go back to work too. She'd been hired for the summer at the CPC cannery. This year she could work legally at the cannery without lying about her age.

The air outside was cool, the moon shone warm and silver through thin clouds. Tatsue finished hanging the wash and looked at the sky through her fingers. Her hands were thin and fragile looking and each oval nail contained the edge of a rising moon. Fred, the boy who walked her home every day after

27

they got off the bus from McKinley High School, said they were refined. She thought Fred was handsome. Otōsan and Okāsan didn't like him.

"His mouth is too big. His lips are too full. Your children will be ugly if you marry him," they said.

Tatsue looked down again at her hands and sighed. She didn't know if they were refined, but she knew they were strong.

She went back to the house and upstairs to her bedroom. She opened her drawer and looked at her apron and gloves and white cannery hairnet. She pulled a glove over her fingers. Tomorrow she would earn fifteen cents an hour as a packer. The man in the window of the payroll office would hand her a numbered pay envelope heavy with silver dollars every week like Otōsan's and Nī-san's. Tatsue lay in bed and drifted off to sleep. She dreamed of buying cotton so sheer it would wear out in a year; she dreamed of wearing dresses that would never have to be handed down.

At five the next morning, the air was damp and smelled cool and sweet. Tatsue made her bento lunch then hurried out of the house and met Edith at the corner.

"Hey, you going work my table this year?" Edith asked as they fell into step together. "If the forelady like us, she keep us on long time. We can make plenty money."

They walked out of Desha Lane down King Street, toward Iwilei and the cannery. Other girls joined them, girls from thirteen to eighteen years old, dressed in homemade dresses, carrying lunch pails, rubber gloves, aprons, and hairnets in their hands. They laughed as they greeted one another. The clouds above the mountains of Nuʻuanu swirled like incense high into the limitless blue sky.

The air at the California Packing Corporation cannery smelled like baked pineapple. It was so thick it clung to Tatsue's skin. The girls walked past the guards through the iron gates into the mechanical landscape. They walked past the trains that brought the pineapple in from the country. Twelve-hour shifts were usual at the peak of the season. Six to six, with one break for lunch.

Tatsue and Edith went to the locker room and put on their caps, gloves, and hairnets. They pinned the *bango* numbers to each other's shoulders.

Edith said, "Last year, I went get sick and my sister took my number and came work for me. The man from the payroll office came with the clipboard and went check the numbers. No check the face. They went pay me anyway. They no care. So long as somebody wear this number. Same thing to them." The cannery paid by the number assigned to a girl when she applied.

The girls walked out into the clatter of the thousands of metal teeth that moved the conveyer belts. The pineapples moved through the cannery on conveyor belts that joined one machine to another like tongues stretched across the room. The pine went from the railroad cars to the Ginaca machine, which chewed them out of most of their skins. The naked pines rode to the trimmers, who picked up the fruit in one hand and with the sharp knives they held in the other hand trimmed out the spots of rind the machine had missed, and the eyes. Tatsue was glad she wasn't a trimmer. Their hands ached from holding the heavy pineapples and their arms were marked with round sores from the pineapple juice dripping down their rubber gloves.

"E, packers! I remember you two from last year, come ova hea to my table," the Portuguese forelady with the loud voice called to them. They followed the pine down the conveyor belt from the trimmers to the slicing machines, where a large, smiling Portuguese woman was standing behind girls packing pineapples into cans.

"You going be first packer this year," the forelady said as she pulled Tatsue into place behind the girl who worked closest to the slicing machine. When the whistle blew, the night crew stopped and Tatsue and Edith stepped up to take their places. The mechanical teeth kept clattering and the pineapple kept flowing endlessly.

The year before, she and Edith had lied about their ages and had come to work scared and silent. They had been afraid of the loud voices of the foreladies. They had been afraid of the machines. But they had made it. Tatsue was proud to be first packer this year.

"No dream, no talk, no take too much time!" the forelady scolded the new girls, but Tatsue and Edith were old timers now.

Tatsue picked out the sweetest slices from the fruit emerging from the slicer and packed them in the small can in front of her. These were the premium pieces and would be sold for the most money. The girls farther down the line picked out the slices that went into cans that were larger and less costly. Broken slices would be fed into machines again and packed into cans to be sold as tidbits, and badly broken pieces would be thrown into mashing machines and pressed for juice.

Tatsue liked being first packer. The pineapple slices came out of the machine clinging neatly together. The vibration of the belt shook them out of their neat arrangement so Tatsue edged closer to the slicing machine to catch the pineapple just as it emerged from the metal mouth. As she settled her body into the clattering mechanical rhythm, she thought of Fred and the wonderful dresses she could make with the money she earned this summer. She would hand Otōsan her pay envelope and he would give her back a few silver dollars to save in her drawer so that she would be able to buy fabric to make new dresses for school. Tatsue could see herself walking home with Fred in her new clothes. "You look like Olivia de Havilland in that dress," he might tell her.

Maybe this year Otōsan would let her go to the movies with Fred. She would lean close to him and he might kiss her, his full lips on hers in a kiss she had seen in the movies at the Waikiki Theatre.

Tatsue reached higher into the mouth of the machine for her next slices. She felt a stinging numbness in her hand. She looked at her glove. The fingertip was open like a mouth trying to scream. She saw the pink flesh around a circle of white bone, all that was left of the tip of her finger.

She bit her lips to pull her mouth smooth and hard across her teeth, so that she would not cry out. The blood-spattered pineapple slices moved down the conveyor belt. Somewhere down the row, Edith began screaming. The girls farther down the line saw the bloody slices and screamed too. Tatsue heard the screaming spread. The screaming echoed down the line, slices to chunks to crushed. The foreladies gathered around Tatsue and swept her off to the dispensary. She did not open her mouth.

At home, she slept. After three days, she still cried silently when her mother changed the bandage. Okāsan thought she was in pain and tried to give her some pills. "No, I no like drink anything."

Otōsan made his impatient face and went downstairs to his chair. Tatsue sank into bed and gathered the soft cotton futon around herself. Her tears sank into the quilt made of dresses she had worn as a small child.

A week after the accident, Tatsue came downstairs to sit at the kitchen table where Okāsan was sewing. Otōsan had been laid off from his carpenter's job at the Libby cannery. He sat in his chair reading his books and smoking the hand-rolled cigarettes he made each morning. Tatsue looked down at her bandaged hand. Now Nī-san was the only one in the household working.

Tatsue left the table and went into the laundry room. She got a bucket and filled the two laundry tubs with water from the furo. It was hard working with one hand but it was dark in the laundry room; no one would see her eyes. There would be no new dresses. The outline of her bandaged finger blurred.

Tatsue put the wooden washboard in one tub and dropped two balls of bluing in the other. She saw the bags of laundry piled on the cement floor. She opened one of the old rice bags that held the boys' dirty laundry. She pulled out Nī-san's crisp new shirt. She pushed it into the water in the first tub, then laid it on the washboard and rubbed the brown bar of soap over it. She moved the shirt up and down over the wooden teeth of the washboard. As she tried to squeeze the soap out of the shirt, she heard someone speak.

"Tatsue."

She looked up, startled. Otōsan was standing in the laundry room. She didn't know how long he had been watching her. She had never seen him in the laundry room before.

"*Sonna koto sen demo ii*, you don't have to do that," Otōsan said softly. Then he took the shirt that she had been washing and twisted it in his carpenter's hands to wring it out. Tatsue watched in amazement as he dipped Nī-san's shirt into the blue rinse water. Otōsan was clumsy and did not rinse like a woman. He invented the motions that he needed to do this task. Tatsue realized he never learned to do this; a Japanese man never washed clothes. The bluing in the water clung to his nails. Each of his nails was grooved so that it looked like the ribbed cotton of his undershirt, tiny ribs running vertically the length of each nail.

"I like that one, you always get that one!" She heard Masao and Kei from beyond the laundry room door and Okāsan's asthmatic coughing that constantly filled the house.

Tatsue watched the yellow carpenter's calluses in Otōsan's palms become gray and soft as he washed his eldest son's shirts in the soapy water. He didn't say anything. He didn't smile at her; he just continued washing and rinsing. Tatsue took the clothes he had finished and fed each piece into the hand-cranked wringer. Otōsan watched her until he was satisfied that the work was light enough for her to do. Then he went back to washing. Tatsue could feel her tears drying, her mouth softening again, her lips rounding into a smile.

Otōsan helped her in the laundry room the whole summer. She loved working silently next to him. He smelled like sawdust, cigarette smoke, and soft gray ashes. They worked through June, July, until it was August, the week before school.

Twelve hands turned the lazy Susan quickly past the vegetables from Okāsan's kitchen garden eager to get a share of the shoyu-cooked fish. The ball bearings Otōsan built into the table under the lazy Susan clattered. It was August, the week before school. Otōsan handed Tatsue three silver dollars.

"That is all that's left, Tatsue." Otōsan said gruffly, avoiding her eyes. "*Shikata ga nakatta*. It couldn't be helped. We had to eat your finger." The table stopped turning. They all stopped eating and stared at him with open mouths. Tatsue did not understand.

"CPC *kara* . . . the cannery paid me money for twelve weeks after your accident. They said 'workman's compensation.' I didn't tell you. I had to use the money to buy food for the whole family."

Tatsue's eyes stung. Mean old man! The cannery had been paying her the entire summer! She pressed her lips hard over her teeth. He had not been able to work. Nī-san's money had not been enough! Otōsan had taken her money and used it. Tatsue looked down at her healing finger. Its tip was gone and it was shorter than the rest. The new nail was growing in wrinkled with tiny ridges.

She thought of Otōsan squatting beside her in the laundry room. A Japanese man does not do women's work. She remembered Otōsan pushing Nī-san's shirts across the wooden ribs of the washboard, the soapy water eating away the hard calluses on his palms and cutting into the deep grooves in his fingernails. He was a practical man. He did not say anything. He did what was necessary. She stared at his fingers as they held out the last three silver dollars he had saved for her.

She looked at Nī-san in his crisp new clothes. He was staring at her finger and she saw his eyes soften then glisten. She looked at the younger boys and her sister Kei in their hand-me-down clothes, at Masao in his new pants made of Otōsan's old work shirt, at Okāsan in her faded dress.

They were staring at her.

"*Shikata ga nai*. Cannot help," she mumbled, words she had been taught. They were as familiar as the offerings she made every evening in a sweet cloud of incense to feed the hungry spirits gathering in the warmth around their family altar.

"*Shikata ga nai*. Cannot help," she said to all of them as they sat together around the kitchen table. And as she said those words, she felt the satisfaction that comes from eating cold rice grains from a small brass dish. It surprised her that she felt nourished and warm. Her family was smiling at her in the last orange light, as the bottoms of the windows filled with the curved edge of the sun.

Tomoe Ame 1959

Forty-five years ago, when I was a kid, my cousin Pam would always get a prize from the Tomoe Ame box that was better than the one I got. If I got a tin whistle, she'd get little glass berries that made a tinkling sound when she shook them. If I got a tiny wooden top, she'd get a wooden *kokeshi* doll with a move-able head. Once, I got a toy car with wheels that turned. She got a little hair ornament with flowers and a fringe of flat tin tassels; she stuck it in her Shirley Temple doll's curly brown hair. Most of the time, she'd position her prizes just out of my reach on her open palm where they'd sparkle in the Hawaiian sun. "See, but don't touch," was what she'd always say to me. It was disgusting.

Tomoe Ame, rice candy, used to come in a two-sectioned box. The large lower section contained fifteen or so pieces of orange candy, gummy and sweet, double wrapped in cellophane and then in tissue-thin rice paper that melted in your mouth. Grandma would say, "Don't eat the first wrapping paper, but you can eat the second one." This confused me because both of the wrappers looked and felt the same. One time, I ate the cellophane wrapper as well as the rice paper wrapper and had a terrible time trying to strip all the bits of cellophane off my tongue. After that, I would carefully unwrap the cellophane wrapper and then try to strip off all of the rice paper wrapping too. I don't remember how old I was when I figured out for sure which wrapper to eat and which to throw away. Tomoe Ame didn't even taste very good. It wasn't sweet and tart like lemon drops, and it didn't have an interesting shape like fish candy or a hole in the middle like Life Savers. In fact, it didn't taste as good as regular American candy that you could get at Fujikawa Store. The only thing that made Tomoe Ame interesting was the small blue second section of the box it came in. This blue section, about one-fourth as long as a matchbox, looked like a little treasure chest. It was sealed shut with a tissue-thin piece of paper with Japanese writing on it. You drew your nail across the seal and opened the box to look at the prize inside.

Tomoe Ame was a treat we got in the summertime. It always arrived in the big brown suitcases carried by the peddler man. He was short and broad and smiled as he walked down the long coral driveway into our camp, which is what we called a group of houses clustered together. He must have come on a regular schedule because our grandmas seemed to know when he would be there. They spread their *goza* mats on the grass in front of my aunt's garage and waited for him to arrive. I remember the garage had unpainted wooden timbers, faced the mountains, and gathered in cool breezes. Our grandmas all looked the same; they wore dresses made of gray or blue fabric printed with tiny flowers. Their hair was rolled into buns at the base of their necks. They sat in a circle on the woven grass mats. They spread patchwork quilts out between them and laid the grandbabies on them. Grandmas sat with their legs sticking straight out or curled to one side beneath their skirts. Their skin was brown and speckled and crinkled like shiny rice paper. They told stories to each other and laughed, bringing up their hands to hide their open mouths.

The peddler man set his suitcases down with a thump in the middle of the grandmothers' circle. Everyone leaned forward as he began to unfasten the big leather buckles and leather straps on his bags. His bags were really a series of nested boxes. On the top layer were shallow trays that held Tomoe Ame, and other Japanese candy. We children liked only the Tomoe Ame. The other kinds of candy were not very good. Some were bland and floury. Others were formed into beautiful flower shapes and painted with soft pinks and greens and golds but after you ate just one piece which tasted like the cotton that collects on the insides of sweater pockets, you were cured from ever wanting to taste another. Our group, the flock of three to six-year-old grandchildren, would huddle around the peddler's box and wait with open mouths as our grandmas began the slow process of getting out coin purses and searching for silver coins to pay for our Tomoe Ame. One by one, we would claim our boxes and swoop out gleefully over the grass, eager to slit the tissue paper seals and see our prizes. The grandmas, freed from our distracting chirping, then began the leisurely inspection of the cases' contents.

We scattered among the hibiscus shrubs, palm trunks, Mickey Mouse berry bushes, and poky fern fronds. I usually went to my favorite place under my aunt's mulberry bush, and there, I opened my blue treasure box. No matter what bright bauble tumbled out into my hand, I knew Pam would have something better. We played with our tiny toys until the fragile pieces broke, probably all of twenty or thirty minutes. Then we would spiral back to the group of women to resume tugging at their skirts and squeaking our high-pitched requests.

But there must have been times when I sat quietly and watched wide-eyed as the cases were unpacked, because I remember seeing some of their contents. There were envelopes, which held tissue paper-wrapped hairnets that were made of filaments so thin that they looked like black spiders' webs. I wondered if they were as strong as the spiders' threads, which my grandpa would wrap around little *ibos*, tiny raised blemishes on the skin. He'd pull the webs tight to cut the tiny tags of skin right off. I remember U-shaped hairpins stuck into cardboard holders, which grandmas used to hold hairnets in place at the napes of their necks and black wax hair coloring crayons, which grandmas used to hide the white stubble that grew in at their hairlines between the times when they would dye their hair. The crayons were big as Grandpa's cigars and I didn't like their greasy dishonest smell. Other envelopes held white powders like *mushi kudashi*, or worm medicine, which a grandma would buy after a number of nights of stinky hunts around a sleepless child's anus. There were miniature glass bottles that held tiny round *jin tan* pills. Grandpa kept the bottles Grandma bought in his *tabako* drawer, next to his pipes and cans of tobacco. There were more mysterious envelopes of powders like *kuma no i* medicine, which if the Japanese name is to be believed, is made out of a bear's stomach. There were *yaito* cones, or moxibustion powders, which could be placed on the skin and lighted if someone had a particularly serious illness. I had heard my uncles say that bad children could also receive a *yaito* treatment, which made me reluctant to ask anything more about it. Cardboard boxes of Salonpas exuded their medicine smell. The women sitting, legs stretched out in the sun, often wore little squares of Salonpas, pasted in longs chains down their calves. The smell of liniment rising from them permeates my childhood.

I remember cards, which were pricked by rows and rows of straight pins and green and purple foil-wrapped packets of sewing needles. Orange and yellow paper wrappers printed with pictures of geishas held oval cakes of olive soap, which I thought was made of green olives. There were celluloid bracelets and pins and earrings made of clusters of Viennese glass flowers and leaves. The women, never interested in jewelry, lost interest in the boxes around this time and began to whisper to each other about illness. Their hands smoothed swollen ankles as they talked in hushed voices about *tonyo byo*, diabetes, *shinzo byo*, heart disease, and *gan*, which is cancer. They nodded sympathetically as each recounted her symptoms, and listened with grave faces as they remembered friends who had already died.

I realize now I don't remember how much money anything cost. I don't know the peddler man's name or how old he was. I don't even know how old the grandmas were or how long they had been getting together. I suspect they had been coming together to talk since the time when the babies that they carried out to their circle were their own. I know these memories are forty-five years old and that all the women were at one time picture brides. I don't know what their hardships were and what plagues they faced, though I know my father had sisters who died of tuberculosis. Some things I've learned in bits and pieces recently, like the reason olive soap was given its name, because it was perfumed by the fragrant olive flower which is called *mokusei* and comes from China. I also realize now that I do not know the Japanese names for sexual things, though the grandmas must have spoken about them because all of them had at least six children. I don't even know when and how all the women died. We moved to a different neighborhood when I was twelve.

I saw a box of Tomoe Ame recently, the treasure box only contains stickers now, the candy company must be afraid of getting sued by parents of children who might choke on small toys. The world has changed. Things come wrapped in plastic and now we drive to shopping centers and supermarkets to buy them. My cousin Pam drives her Mercedes, and I drive my Ford; we don't have time to drive to places where we can meet and sit together.

But I am over fifty now and sometime, I'd like to sit on the grass for an hour in front of a garage made of unpainted wooden timbers that collects cool mountain breezes like an open palm. I 'd like to whisper about cancer and diabetes or even the waning of sexual things. I could call Pam and ask if she'd like to talk, but I know she is too busy. She has an internet fashion business to run.

Sometimes I wonder if the peddler man is still alive. I wonder what happened to his wonderful nested treasure boxes.

Grandfather 1955

I never told you that I loved you.
There is no word for that
in your Japanese
between grandfather and child.

If I had told you in my English
you would have smiled.
It would not have touched your heart.

I had only my English,
that language of plantation *luna*,
words smelling of vinegar and animal flesh
that hurled themselves down in short angry bursts
upon the backs of Japanese men
hoeing endless rows in canefields.
I had only my English,
words that sifted out of pay envelopes
like the red dust of the plantations,
words that settled into spaces
left by money withheld
by the company store.
I had only my English,
language of cannery foremen.

I wish I could have given you
words of deference and honor
words clinging together, fat and sweet
like white rice
on yellow brass plates
we gave to the household shrine
each day at dusk.
I wish I could have offered you
words from your lost Japan,
smooth and round and as full of honey

as the orange persimmons we set
on little wooden platforms
for the ancestors.

For you taught me
to love the green breath of orchids,
to hear the sighs of the leaves,
to bow with reverence
to the rising sun.
I never told you I loved you,
I had no word.

Now I will sit at the altar
I will strike the small brass gong
I will light three sticks of incense
and watch the blue smoke rise.

If I set a match to this paper
perhaps it will whisper
as it gives itself to the yellow flames,
whisper these meanings to the blue smoke,
whisper them to you.

Taiko **Drums**

Bon Odori, the dance of summer
danced to the rhythm beaten
from the belly of the *taiko* drum.

Beaten by a man on bamboo scaffolding high above,
drum beats round, like the disk of the moon,
drum beats so low they hum circles into my bones.

I was twelve
the first time I moved
to the *taiko*'s beat.
The first time I danced
enfolded in cotton *yukata* in a woman's *shibui* colors,
turned my toes inward,
claimed the right to a woman's modest steps.
I moved my hands in the warm summer air
caught the heavy, ripe outline
of the moon in my fingers,
felt it rippling down the skin of my arms,
collected its pools of cool silver
within my sleeves.

I was twelve the first time I followed
the *taiko*'s deep bellied beat.
Danced my first
circles into the soft blackness of the night,
felt the rhythm beaten by a man
reverberating in my bones.

Carnival Queen

My friend Terry and I both have boys' nicknames. But that's the only thing about us that is the same. Terry is beautiful. She is about 5'4" tall, which is tall enough to be a stewardess. I am only 5' tall, which is too short, so I should know.

My mother keeps asking me why Terry is my friend. This makes me nervous, because I really don't know. Ever since we had the first senior class officers' meeting at my house and my mother found the empty Tampax container in our wastebasket she has been really asking a lot of questions about Terry. Terry and I are the only girls who were elected to office. She's treasurer and I'm secretary. The president, the vice-president, and the sergeant-at-arms are all boys. I guess that's why Terry and I hang out together. Like when we have to go to class activities and meetings, she picks me up. I never even knew her before we were elected. I don't know who she used to hang around with, but it sure wasn't with me and my friends. We're too Japanese girl—you know—plain. I mean, Terry has skin like a porcelain doll. She has cheekbones like Garbo, a body like Ann Margaret, she has legs like, well, not like any Japanese girl I've ever seen. Like I said, she's beautiful. She always dresses perfectly, too. She always wears an outfit, a dress with matching straw bag and colored leather shoes. Her hair is always set, combed, and sprayed; she even wears nylon stockings under her jeans, even on really hot days. Terry is the only girl I know who has her own Liberty House charge card. Not that she ever goes shopping by herself. Whenever she goes near a store, her mother goes with her.

Funny, Terry has this beautiful face, perfect body, and nobody hates her. We hate Valerie. Valerie is the only girl in our P.E. class who can come out of the girls' showers, wrap a towel around herself under her arms and have it stay up by itself. No hands. She always takes the longest time in the showers and walks back to her locker past the rest of us, who are already dry and fumbling with the one hook on the back of our bras. Valerie's bra has five hooks on the back of it and needs all of them to stay closed. I think she hangs that thing across the top of her locker door on purpose just so we can walk past it and be blinded by it shining in the afternoon sun. One time, my friend Tina got fed up and snatched Val's bra. She wore it on top of her head and ran around the locker room. I swear, she looked like an albino Mickey Mouse. Nobody did anything but laugh. Funny, it was Terry who took the bra away and put it back on Val's locker again.

I don't know why we're friends, but I wasn't surprised when we ended up together as contestants in the Carnival Queen contest. The Carnival Queen contest is a tradition at McKinley. They have pictures of every Carnival Queen ever chosen hanging in the auditorium corridor right next to the pictures of the senators, governors, politicians, and millionaires who graduated from the school. This year there are already five portraits of queens up there. All the girls are wearing long ball gowns and the same rhinestone crown, which is placed on their heads by Mr. Harano, the principal. They have elbow-length white gloves and they're carrying baby's breath and roses. The thing is, all the girls are *hapa*. Every one.

Every year, it is the same tradition. A big bunch of girls gets nominated to run, but everybody knows from intermediate school on, which girl in the class is actually going to win. She has to be *hapa*.

"They had to nominate me," I try to tell Terry. "I'm a class officer, but you, you actually have a chance to be the only Japanese girl to win." Terry had just won the American Legion essay contest the week before. You would think that being fashionable and coordinated all the time would take all her energy and wear her out, but her mother wants her to be smart too. She looks at me with this sad face I don't understand.

"I doubt it," she says.

Our first orientation meeting for contestants is today in the library after school. I walk to the meeting actually glad to be there after class. The last after-school meeting I went to was the one I was forced to attend. That one had no contestants. Just potential school dropouts. The first meeting, I didn't know anybody there. Nobody I know in the student government crowd is like me and has actually flunked chemistry. All the guys, who were coming in the door, were the ones who hang around the bathrooms that I'm too scared to use. Nobody ever threatened me though, and after a while, dropout class wasn't half bad, but I have to admit I like this meeting better. I sit down and watch the other contestants come through the door. I know the name of almost every girl who walks in. Terry is there, of course, wearing a blue suede jumper, silk blouse, navy stockings, and navy patent leather shoes. My friend Trudye, who has a great figure for an Oriental girl, wears braces and coke bottle glasses. My friend Linda, who has a beautiful face but a basic *musubi*-shaped body; the Yanagawa twins, who have beautiful *hapa* faces, but, pretty tragic, they inherited their father's genes and have government-issue Japanese girl legs. Song-

leaders, cheerleaders, ROTC sponsors, student government committee heads;
I know them all. Krissie Clifford, who is small and blonde, comes running in
late. Krissie looks like a young version of Beaver's mother on the TV show.
She's always running like she just fell out of the screen, and if she moves fast
enough, she can catch up with the TV world and jump back in. Then *she* walks
in. Leilani Jones. As soon as she walks in the door, everybody in the room turns
to look at her. Everybody in the room knows that Leilani is the only girl who
can win.

As soon as Leilani walks in, Mrs. Takahara, the teacher advisor, says, "Well
now, take your seats everyone. We can begin."

We each take a wooden chair on either side of two rows of long library
tables. There is a makeup kit and mirror at each of the places. Some of Mrs.
Takahara's friends who are teachers are also sitting in.

"This is Mrs. Chung, beauty consultant of Kamedo cosmetics," Mrs.
Takahara says. "She will show us the proper routines of skin cleansing and
makeup. The Carnival Queen contest is a very special event. All the girls who
are contestants must be worthy representatives of McKinley High School. This
means the proper makeup and attitude. Mrs. Chung . . ."

I have to admire the beauty consultant. Even though her makeup is obvious as scaffolding in front of a building, it is so well done, kind of like the men
who dance the girls' parts in Kabuki shows, you look at it and actually believe
that what you are seeing is her face.

"First, we start with proper cleansing," she says. We stare into our own
separate mirrors.

"First, we pin our hair so that it no longer hangs in our faces." All of the
girls dig in handbags and come up with bobby pins. Hairstyles disappear as
we pin our hair straight back. The teachers look funny, kind of young without
their teased hair. Mrs. Chung walks around to each station. She squeezes a glop
of pink liquid on a cotton ball for each of us.

"Clean all the skin well," she says. "Get all the dirt and impurities out."
We scrub hard with that cotton ball; we all know that our skin is loaded with
lots of stuff that is impure. My friend Trudye gets kind of carried away. She
scrubs so hard around her eyes that she scrubs off her Scotch tape. She hurries
over to Mrs. Takahara's chair, mumbles something and excuses herself. I figure
she'll be gone pretty long. The only bathroom that is safe for us to use is all the
way over in the other building.

"Now we moisturize," Mrs. Chung is going on. "We use this step to correct defects in the tones of our skins." I look over at Terry. I can't see any defects in any of the tones of her skin.

"This mauve moisturizer corrects sallow undertones," Mrs. Chung says.

"What's 'shallow'?" I whisper to Terry.

"'Sallow'," she whispers back, disgusted. "Yellow."

"Oh," I say and gratefully receive the large glop of purple stuff Mrs. Chung is squeezing on my new cotton ball. Mrs. Chung squeezes a little on Terry's cotton ball too. When she passes Lani, she smiles and squeezes white stuff out from a different tube.

I happily sponge the purple stuff on. Terry is sponging too but I notice she is beginning to look like she has the flu. "Next, foundation," says Mrs. Chung. She is walking around, narrowing her eyes at each of us and handing us each a tube that she is sure is the correct color to bring out the best in our skin. Mrs. Chung hands me a plastic tube of dark beige. She gives Terry a tube of lighter beige and gives Lani a different tube altogether.

"Just a little translucent crème." She smiles to Lani who smiles back rainbow bubbles and strands of pearls.

Trudye comes rushing back and Linda catches her up on all the steps she's missed. I got to admit, without her glasses and with all that running, she has really pretty cheekbones and nice colored skin. I notice she has new Scotch tape on too, and is really concentrating on what Mrs. Chung is saying next.

"Now that we have the proper foundation, we concentrate on the eyes." She pulls out a rubber and chrome pincer machine. She stands in front of Linda with it. I become concerned.

"The eyelashes sometimes grow in the wrong direction," Mrs. Chung informs us. "They must be trained to bend correctly. We use the eyelash curler to do this." She hands the machine to Linda. I watch as Linda puts the metal pincer up to her eye and catches her straight, heavy black lashes between the rubber pincer blades.

"Must be sore if they do it wrong and squeeze the eyelid meat," I breathe to Terry. Terry says nothing. She looks upset, like she is trying not to bring up her lunch.

"Eyeshadow must be applied to give the illusion of depth," says Mrs. Chung. "Light on top of the lid, close to the lashes, luminescent color on the whole lid, a dot of white in the center of the lid, and brown below the brow bone to accentuate the crease." Mrs. Chung is going pretty fast now. I wonder what the girls who have Oriental eyelids without a crease are going to do. I check out the room quickly over the top of my makeup mirror. Sure enough, all the Oriental girls here have a nice crease in their lids. Those who don't are wearing Scotch tape. Mrs. Chung is passing out "pearlescent" eyeshadow.

"It's made of fish scales," Terry says. I have eyelids that are all right, but eyeshadow, especially sparkling eyeshadow, makes me look like a gecko, you know, with protruding eye sockets that go in separate directions. Terry has beautiful deep-socketed eyes and brow bones that don't need any help to look well defined. I put on the stuff in spite of my better judgment and spend the rest of the time trying not to move my eyeballs too much, just in case anybody notices. Lani is putting on all this makeup too. But in her case, it just increases the pearly glow that her skin is already producing.

"This ends the makeup session," Mrs. Chung says. "Now our eyes and skins have the proper preparation for our roles as contestants for Carnival Queen."

"Ma, I running in the Carnival Queen contest," I was saying last night. My mother got that exasperated look on her face.

"You think you get chance!"

"No, but the teachers put in the names of all the student council guys." My mother was beginning to look like she was suffering again.

"When you were small, everybody used to tell me you should run for Cherry Blossom contest. But that was before you got so dark like your father. I always tell you no go out in the sun or wear lotion like me when you go out but you never listen."

"Yeah, Ma, but we get modeling lessons, makeup, how to walk."

"Good, might make you stand up straight. I would get you a back brace, but when you were small, we paid so much money for your legs, to get special shoes connected to a bar. You cried and never would wear them. That's why you still have crooked legs."

That was last night. Now I'm here and Mrs. Takahara is telling us about walking and modeling lessons. "Imagine a string coming out of the top of your skull and connected to the ceiling. Shorten the string and walk with your chin out and back erect. Float! Put one foot in front of the other, point your toes outward and glide forward on the balls of your feet. When you stop, place one foot slightly behind the other at a forty-five degree angle. Put your weight on the back foot." I should have worn the stupid shoes when I was small. I'm bowlegged. Just like my father. Leilani is not bowlegged. She looks great putting one long straight tibia in front of the other. I look kind of like a crab. We walk in circles around and around the room. Terry is definitely not happy. She's walking pretty far away from me. Once, when I pass her, I can swear she is crying.

"Wow, long practice, yeah?" I say as we walk across the lawn heading toward the bus. Terry, Trudye, Linda, and I are still together. A black Buick pulls up to the curb. Terry's mom has come to pick her up. Terry's mom always picks her up. She must have just come back from the beauty shop. Her head is wrapped in a new pink wind bonnet. Kind of like the cake we always get at weddings that my mother keeps on top of the television and never lets anybody eat.

"I'll call you," Terry says.

"I'm so glad that you and Theresa do things together," Terry's mother says. "Theresa needs girlfriends like you, Sam." I'm looking at the new pink bonnet around her face. I wonder if Terry's father ever gets the urge to smash her hair down to feel the shape of her head. Terry looks really uncomfortable as they drive away.

I feel uncomfortable too. Trudye and Linda's makeup looks really weird in the afternoon sunlight. My eyeballs feel larger than tank turrets and they must be glittering brilliantly too. The Liliha-Puʻunui bus comes and we all get on. The long center aisle of the bus gives me an idea. I put one foot in front of the other and practice walking down. Good thing it is late and the guys we go to school with are not getting on.

"You think Leilani is going to win?" Trudye asks.

"What?" I say as I almost lose my teeth against the metal pole I'm holding on to. The driver has just started up and standing with your feet at a forty-five degree angle doesn't work on public transportation.

"Lani is probably going to win, yeah?" Trudye says again. She can hide her eye makeup behind her glasses and looks pretty much okay. "I'm going to stay in for the experience. Plus, I'm going to the orthodontist and take my braces out, and I asked my mother if I could have contact lenses and she said okay." Trudye goes on, but I don't listen. I get a seat by the window and spend the whole trip looking out so nobody sees my fish-scale eyes.

I am not surprised when I get home and the phone begins to ring.

"Sam, it's Terry. You stay in the contest. But I decided I'm not going to run."

"That's nuts Terry," I half scream at her. "You are the only one of us besides Lani that has a chance to win. You could be the first Japanese Carnival Queen that McKinley ever has." I am going to argue this one.

"Do you know the real name of this contest?" Terry asks.

"I don't know, Carnival Queen. I've never thought about it, I guess."

"It's the Carnival Queen Scholarship Contest."

"Oh, so?" I'm still interested in arguing that only someone with legs like Terry even has a chance.

"Why are you running? How did you get nominated?" Terry asks.

"I don't know, I guess because I used to write poems for English class and they always got in the paper or the yearbook. And probably because Miss Chuck made me write a column for the newspaper for one year to bring up my social studies grade."

"See . . . and why am I running?" Terry continues.

"Okay, you're class officer, and sponsor, and you won the American Legion essay contest . . . ."

"And Krissie?"

"She's editor of the yearbook and a sponsor, and the Yanagawa twins are song leaders and committee chairmen, and Trudye is prom committee chairman, and Linda..." I am getting into it.

"And Lani," Terry says quietly.

"Well, she's a sponsor, I think . . . ." I've lost some momentum. I really don't know.

"I'm a sponsor, and I know she's not one," Terry says.

"Student government? No . . . I don't think so . . . not cheering, her sister is the one in the honor society, not . . . hey, not, couldn't be . . ."

"That's right," Terry says. "The only reason she's running is because she's supposed to win." It can't be true. "That means the rest of us are all running for nothing. The best we can do is second place." My ears are getting sore with the sense of what she says. "We're running because of what we did. But we're going to lose because of what we look like. Look, it's still good experience and you can still run if you like."

"Nah . . . ." I say, still dazed by it. "But what about Mrs. Takahara, what about your mother?" Terry is quiet.

"I think I can handle Mrs. Takahara," Terry finally says.

"I'll say I'm not running too. If it's two of us, it won't be so bad." I am actually kind of relieved that this is the last day I'll have to put gecko-eye makeup all over my face.

"Thanks Sam," Terry says.

"Yeah . . . . My mother will actually be relieved. Ever since I forgot the ending at my piano recital in fifth grade, she gets really nervous if I'm in front of any audience."

"You want me to pick you up for the carnival Saturday night?" Terry asks.

"I'll ask my mom," I say. "See you then . . . ."

"Yeah . . . ."

I think, *We're going to lose because of what we look like.* I need a shower, my eyes are itching anyway. I'm glad my mother isn't home yet. I think best in the shower and sometimes I'm in there an hour or more.

Soon, in a world that's a small square of warm steam and tile walls, it all starts going through my head. The teachers looked so young in the makeup demonstration with their hair pinned back—they looked kind of like us. But we are going to lose because of what we look like. I soap the layers of makeup off my face. I guess they're tired of looking like us; *musubi* bodies, *daikon* legs, *furoshiki*-shaped homemade dresses, *bento* tins to be packed in the early mornings, mud and sweat everywhere. The water is splashing down on my face and hair. But Krissie doesn't look like us, and she is going to lose too. Krissie looks like the Red Cross society lady from intermediate school. She looks like Beaver's mother on the television show. Too *haole*. She's going to lose because of the way she looks. Lani doesn't look like anything from the past. She looks like something that could only have been born underwater where all motions are slow and all sounds are soft. I turn off the water and towel off. Showers always make me feel clean and secure. I guess I can't blame even the teachers, everyone wants to feel safe and secure.

My mother is sitting at the table peeling an orange. She does this almost every night and I already know what she's going to say.

"Eat this orange, good for you, lots of vitamin C."

"I don't want to eat orange now, Ma." I know it is useless, but I say it anyway. My mother is the kind of Japanese lady who will hunch down real small when she passes in front of you when you're watching TV. Makes you think

48

she's quiet and easygoing, but not on the subject of vitamin C.

"I peeled it already. Make yourself want it." Some people actually think my mother is shy.

"I not running in the contest. Terry and I going quit."

"Why?" my mother asks, like she really doesn't need to know.

"Terry said that we running for nothing. Everybody already knows Lani going win." My mother looks like she just tasted some orange peel.

"That's not the real reason." She hands me the orange and starts washing the dishes.

There's lots of things I don't understand. Like why Terry hangs out with me. Why my mother is always so curious about her and now why she doesn't think this is the real reason that Terry is quitting the contest.

"What did the mother say about Terry quitting the contest?" my mother asks without turning around.

"I donno, nothing I guess."

"Hmm . . . that's not the real reason. That girl is different. The way the mother treats her is different." Gee, having a baby and being a mother must be really hard and it must really change a person because all I know is that my mother is really different from me.

Terry picks me up Saturday night in her brother's white Mustang. It's been a really busy week. I haven't even seen her since we quit the contest. We had to build the Senior Class Starch Throwing booth.

"Hi, Sam. We're working until ten o'clock on the first shift, okay?" Terry is wearing a triangle denim scarf in her hair, a workshirt, and jeans. Her face is flushed from driving with the Mustang's top down and she looks really glamorous.

"Yeah, I thought we weren't going to finish the booth this afternoon. Lucky thing my dad and Lenny's dad helped us with the hammering and Valerie's committee got the cardboard painted in time. We kind of ran out of workers because most of the girls . . ." I don't have to finish. Most of the student council girls are getting dressed for the contest.

"Mrs. Sato and the cafeteria ladies finished cooking the starch, and Neal and his friends and some of the football guys are going to carry the big pots of starch over to the booth for us." Terry is in charge of the manpower because she knows everybody.

"Terry's mother is on the phone!" my mother calls to us from the house. Terry runs in to answer the phone. Funny, her mother always calls my house when Terry is supposed to pick me up. My mother looks out at me from the door. The look on her face says, "Checking up." Terry runs past her and jumps back in the car.

"You're lucky, your mother is really nice," she says.

We go down Kuakini Street and turn onto Liliha. We pass School Street and head down the freeway on-ramp. Terry turns on KPOI and I settle down in my seat. Terry drives faster than my father. We weave in and out of cars as she guns the Mustang down H-1. I know this is not very safe, but I like the feeling in my stomach. It's like going down hills. My hair is flying wild and I feel so clean and good. Like the first day of algebra class before the symbols get mixed up. Like the first day of chemistry before we have to learn molar solutions. I feel like it's going to be the first day forever so I can make the clean feeling last and last. The ride is too short. We turn off by the Board of Water Supply station and we head down by the Art Academy and turn down Pensacola past Mr. Feirerra's green gardens and into the parking lot of the school.

"I wish you were still in the contest tonight," I tell Terry as we walk out toward the carnival grounds. "I mean you are so perfect for the Carnival Queen. You were the only Japanese girl that was perfect enough to win."

"I thought you were my friend," Terry mumbles. "You sound like my mother. You only like me because of what you think I should be." She starts walking faster and is leaving me behind.

"Wait! What? How come you getting so mad?" I'm running to keep up with her.

"Perfect, perfect. What if I'm *not* perfect? What if I'm not what people think I am? What if I can't be what people think I am?" She's not making any sense to me and she's crying. "Why can't you just like me? I thought you were different. I thought you were my friend because you just like *me*." I'm following her and I feel like it's exam time in chemistry. I'm flunking again and I don't understand.

We get to the senior booth and Terry disappears behind the cardboard. Valerie from P.E. is there and hands me a lot of paper cupcake cups and a cafeteria juice ladle.

"Quick, we need at least a hundred of these filled with starch; we're going to be open in ten minutes."

"Try wait, I got to find Terry." I look behind the cardboard back of the booth. Terry is not there. I run all around the booth. Terry is nowhere in sight. The senior booth is under a tent in the midway with all the games. There are lots of light bulbs strung like kernels of corn on wires inside the tent. There are lots of game booths and rows and rows of stuffed animal prizes on clotheslines above each booth. I can't find Terry and I want to look around more, but all of a sudden the merry-go-round music starts and all the lights come on. The senior booth with its hand-painted signs, "Starch Throw—three scrip" looks alive all of a sudden in the warm carnival light.

"Come on, Sam!" Valerie is calling me. "We're opening. I need you to help!" I go back to the booth. Pretty soon Terry comes back and I look at her kind of worried, but under the soft popcorn light, I cannot even tell she has been crying.

"Terry, Mr. Miller said that you're supposed to watch the scrip can and take it to the cafeteria when it's full," Val says to her, blocking my view. Some teachers are arriving for first shift. They need to put on shower caps and stick their heads through holes in the cardboard so students can buy paper cupcake cups full of starch to throw to try to hit the teachers' faces. Terry goes in the back to help the teachers get ready. Lots of guys from my drop-out class are lining up in the front of the booth.

"Eh, Sam, come on take my money. Ogawa's back there. He gave me the F in math. Gimme the starch!" Business is getting better by the minute. Me, Val, and Terry are running around the booth, taking scrip, filling cupcake cups, and getting out of the way fast when the guys throw the starch. Pretty soon, the grass in the middle of the booth turns into a mess that looks like a starch swamp, and we are trying not to slip as we run around trying to keep up with business.

"Ladies and gentlemen, McKinley High School is proud to present the 1966 Carnival Queen and her court." It comes over the loudspeaker. It must be the end of the contest, ten o'clock. All the guys stop buying starch and turn to look toward the front of the tent. Pretty soon, everyone in the tent has cleared the center aisle. They clap as five girls in evening dresses walk our way.

Oh, great, I think. *I have starch in my hair and I don't want to see them.* The girls are all dressed in long gowns and are wearing white gloves. The first girl is Linda. She looks so pretty in a maroon velvet A-line gown. Cannot see her *musubi*-shaped body and her face is just glowing. The rhinestones in her tiara are sparkling under each of the hundreds of carnival lights. The ribbon across her chest says "Third Princess." It's neat! Just like my cousin Carolyn's wedding. My toes are tingling under their coating of starch. The next is Trudye. She's not wearing braces and she looks so pretty in her lavender gown. Some of the guys are going "Wow" under their breath as she walks by. The first Princesses pass next, the Yanagawa twins. They're wearing matching pink gowns and have pink baby roses in their hair, which is in ringlets. Their tiaras look like lace snowflakes on their heads as they pass by. And last. Even though I know who this is going to be I really want to see her. Lani's white dress looks like it is made of sugar crystals. As she passes, her crown sparkles tiny rainbows under the hundreds of light bulbs from the tent and the flashbulbs popping like little suns.

The court walks through the crowd and stops at the senior booth. Mr. Harano, the principal, steps out.

"Your majesty," he says to Lani, who is really glowing. "I will become a target in the senior booth in your honor. Will you and your Princesses please take aim and do your best as royal representatives of our school?"

I look around at Terry. The principal is acting so stupid. I can't believe he really runs the whole school. Terry must be getting so sick. But I look at her and she's standing in front of Lani and smiling. This is weird. She's the one who said the contest was fixed. She's the one who said everyone knows who was supposed to win. She's smiling at Lani like my grandmother used to smile at me when I was five. Like I was a sweet *mochi* dumpling floating in red bean soup. I cannot stand it. I quit the contest so she wouldn't have to quit alone. And she yells at me and hasn't talked to me all night. All I wanted was for her to be standing there instead of Lani.

The Carnival Queen and four Princesses line up in front of the booth. Val, Terry, and I scramble around giving each of them three cupcake cups of starch. They get ready to throw. The guys from the newspaper and the yearbook get ready to take their picture. I lean as far back into the wall as I can. I know Trudye didn't have time to get contacts yet and she's not wearing any glasses. I wonder where Val is and if she can flatten out enough against the wall to get out of the way. Suddenly, a hand reaches out and grabs my ankle. I look down, and Terry, who is sitting under the counter of the booth with Val, grabs my hand and pulls me down on the grass with them. The ground here is nice and clean. The Carnival Queen and Princesses and the rows of stuffed animals are behind and above us. The air is filled with pink cupcake cups and starch as they throw. Mr. Harano closes his eyes, the flashbulbs go off, no one comes close to hitting his face. Up above us, everyone is laughing and clapping. Down below, Terry, Val and I are nice and clean.

"Lani looks so pretty, Sam." Terry is looking at me and smiling.

"Yeah, even though the contest was juice she looks really good. Like a storybook," I say, hoping it's not sounding too fake.

"Thanks for quitting with me." Terry's smile is like the water that comes out from between the rocks at Kunawai Stream. I feel so clean in that smile.

"It would have been lonely if I had to quit by myself," Terry says, looking down at our starch-covered shoes. And even if I'm covered with starch, I know that to her, I am beautiful. Her smile tells me that we're friends because I went to drop-out class. It is a smile that can wash away all the F's that Mr. Low, my chemistry teacher, will ever give. I have been waiting all my life for my mother to give me that smile. I know it is a smile that Terry's mother has never smiled at her. I don't know where she learned it.

It's quiet now. The Carnival Queen and her Princesses have walked away. Terry stands up first as she and Val and I start to crawl out from our safe place under the counter of the booth. She gives me her hand to pull me up and I can see her out in the bright carnival light. Maybe every girl looks like a queen at one time in her life.

Pretend

The homecoming game is tomorrow. Nathan, Lenny, you, and me at 3 a.m. are still sitting on the back of a flatbed truck building the sign for the senior class float: KRUSH KAMEHAMEHA.

Sitting under a papier-mâché tiger after ten hours, wiring tissue paper flowers to a chicken-wire frame. The rest of the committee went home at twelve o'clock when the Hawaiian policeman in the blue Oldsmobile came cruising.

"You guys playing Kamehameha," he smiled. "No use paint that tiger black and gold, might as well paint 'em black and blue."

Now it's only us still sitting and tying Kleenex flowers, senior class officers and homecoming chairman.

"Homecoming! How come we gotta play Kam? We never going beat Kam."

"How come we not playing Kalani?"

"Maybe they thought was Kam's homecoming."

"Maybe Kam going pretend it *is* their homecoming."

I sink down into a pile of flowers. "Come on, you guys," I whine. "Shut up! Mr. Miller said we have to finish this float. Shame if we're the only class without a float."

Beyond our lighted flatbed island, Mrs. Clower's English building looks different flickering in blue-gray, television-colored moonlight. The shadows have been rising like high tide since midnight and look wet clinging to buildings. The darkness puddled on the grass is damp and smells salty like ocean water or tears.

You twist the wire tail of another flower into place right next to my hand. Your hair is sun-streaked from surfing, your skin is brown as dried ginger root. I have been watching you secretly all year. Your laugh is gentle as a shorebreak little kids can play in. I sit next to you and dream. Maybe if I could go to Ala Moana beach with you, I could change from being one of the girls sitting on the sand all day hiding my thighs under a beach towel to somebody who gets to ride a surfboard all the way out to the reef. I know your real name, but ever since the time you had to get your hair cut short for ROTC in sophomore year, the guys all call you "Wana," which means 'prickly sea urchin.'

You smile, "Shhhhh . . ." at me then slip off the back end of the flatbed, disappear into the night and surface into moonlight twenty yards away. You run up the steps of the English building quadrangle, dripping darkness, smiling secrets. You lift a finger, take careful aim, and say "Pa Kew!" so real I can hear the bullet spinning out of the imaginary barrel of your finger. Then "Pock," you throw a wadded up paper flower at the back of Nathan's head.

"Wana, you sucka!" Nathan explodes and whirls toward you. He and Lenny dive off the flatbed as you smile John Wayne at me and roll into a curving patch of shadow.

Lenny and Nathan surface in gray moonlight and—

"Krack."

"Brang."

"Ka choom!"

They unleash a hail of paper flower bullets at your hiding place. You surface and take each tiny impact with arms out wild like you're falling off your board, and begin a spiral to the grass so real I scream. You roll out of sight. Nathan and Lenny get the "pretty soon cannot touch bottom" tingle as they slip deeper into darkness to hunt for you. Sergeant Saunders, Marshall Dillon, they creep into the shadows. I can see they are almost on top of you as you lie still, head and chest covered with shadows, like starfish under sand.

Then you explode up, Elliot Ness semi-automatic burp gun firing paper flower bullets blazing. Lenny and Nathan, splashed in surprise, yelling, "No fair, you *make*, you sucka." But you're screaming like rapid fire bursts between machine gun rounds.

"New man!" As you mow them down. And we're laughing so hard like sand in eyes, we cannot see; we're laughing until like water coming out through nose, we cannot breathe. Until we cannot hear, ears stuck with laughter, but you're screaming at us anyway, triumphant, "New man! New man!"

Next day, first time in history, we actually beat Kam. It is only three weeks later I call Lenny to tell him I heard it on the news. Your car turned over in the canal, you pinned inside. His words break over me.

"Fuck you, no lie, no lie!"

And now in this room the smell of incense and flowers is so thick and the priest is chanting so slow it's like moving through water. The light is rose pink to make the colors in your face look real so we can pretend you're sleeping. I watch your mother and I'm surprised she's so much younger than mine. She's crying, she's catching her tears in a piece of white Kleenex. I walk up to say goodbye to you, one of a hundred of your classmates.

"I cannot say Namu Amida Butsu! I started going to Nuuanu Church, I'm Christian," I whisper to Lenny.

"Just pretend," he hisses back at me. "Just pretend."

The priest hits a bronze bowl gong with a hard wooden mallet. The sound rushes out at us then folds back around itself, making a hollow, a tube, smooth and long as a blue-green wave. I walk up to the urn and pick up the pieces of incense that feel like grains of sand. I bow silently as I sprinkle them on to the burning embers. I look at your face, but I can't say anything. From now on, I know it's going to be hard to pretend.

Thinking of an Octopus

Lots of times
when I was a kid,
my father would come home from fishing
pull a fresh caught octopus
out of its last safety,
an old rice bag,
bang it down into the washtub,
throw on a handful of Hawaiian salt
and scrub the mucus and most of the life
out of its soft tender skin.
Then he threw the dazed bunch of jelly
into a cold metal colander
and into the icebox
while he finished unpacking his fishing stuff,
washing the boat,
sharpening his knives.

The octopus usually died there,
in that cold icebox
its air all gone
salt stinging,
cold numbing its brain.
But sometimes I would open the door
and I would see it,
its eyes glassy and dead.

But I could tell it was alive.
Its skin was still trying
to match the rippling beige sands
of the ocean bottom,
red patches of seaweed
it was hiding in this morning,
the gray rolling eternal of
a sky of ocean,

pierced by tentacles of sunlight.
The octopus's skin
still moving with the rhythm
and color and textures of its life in the sea.
Trying hard even now
for that combination
that always before bought it safety,
that always before set it free.
They'd yell at me
to shut the icebox door
and I'd cry.
But I don't cry anymore.
Even though tomorrow
is my 36th birthday and I'm lying here dazed,
in the air conditioned chill,
right before surgery.
Two weeks of the words 'breast cancer'
have flayed away my skin.
I'm punctured with tubes,
strapped down to this
stainless steel table.
Across the moist surface of my brain,
The Lord's Prayer, Hail Marys
and the Nembutsu keep fluttering;
rippling across my brain
with the picture
of an octopus.

Chemotherapy

The slightest touch in the shower and my hair pulls out of my scalp, coming out in my fingers in wide black ribbons. The ribbons flow down my back and arms with the warm water. They encircle me, cling to the warmth of my body like a toddler fearful of being left. Finally, curling in tendrils around my ankles, they flow reluctantly toward the drain. There, abandoned by water, and trapped against the silvery round grating, they twist themselves into black balls, hollow worlds, empty nests.

Medical Report:
    Patient is a 35 y/o who had surgery on July 18 for CA of lt breast. The operative findings showed infiltrating ductile CA w/ productive fibrosis, stage II. Pt is pre menopausal.

"Cancer patients are usually the most agreeable people," the medical social worker informed me before my first chemotherapy session. "They are viewed by their families and co-workers as uncomplaining selfless saints who give up everything for others. Cancer survivors, on the other hand, are difficult." She paused, eyeing me slowly. "They laugh when they need to laugh, cry when they need to cry, demand what they need and don't ask permission."

The chemotherapy agent is a chemical cocktail that goes directly into a vein in my arm. This perverse happy hour will continue weekly for one full year. My cousin Taeko drives me to my first treatment. She is twenty years older than I, a retired accountant. She volunteered for the job. I was never close to her, and I ponder the mystery. The nurses in the oncology unit are professionally cheerful. They give me a round yellow pill in a small paper cup. "For the nausea, that may come," they explain. I swallow the Compazine and escape the chemotherapy room, which is called a cell. My cousin and I walk across the street to Thomas Square. Under the giant trees, I wait for the tiny sphere of calm to unravel in the pit of my stomach.

"I wanted to drive you because you look like my mother," my cousin, who is old enough to have been my mother, explains. Then I remember. The dark woman in the photo. Thin and fragile, with deep-set eyes. The one that all my life people have begun sentences about, "You look just like Big Auntie," before averting their eyes and looking hurriedly away. I want to respond but the Compazine has dissolved. Tranquility has unrolled within me; it spreads out and settles languidly, it weighs down my tongue.

I return to the chemotherapy cell, a bright chamber with impervious surfaces. My thoughts unreel but bypass speech. The nurses swab my arm and in the hollow above the bones of my elbow, they insert a tiny needle that feels like the ember of a strand of spider web singeing the surface of my skin. The kindly-faced nurse opens a clamp, and I feel a surge of unexpected cool, like the north wind on a summer day, or the bubbling of artesian water out of the mouth of Kunawai Stream.

"First we just run saline through the lines," the nurse is explaining, "to buffer the chemicals." I drift in the cool, thinking of the strands of algae waving at the bottom of the stream bed in Kunawai Park, and I hear the stories about the thin dark woman who was confined at Palama Settlement with tuberculosis eating away at her lungs. She pounded the heads of her children, saying, "You better be good, you better study, you . . ." until they no longer wanted to go see her and ran off into the neighboring vegetable gardens on visiting days.

"Here come the chemicals now," comes the announcement, as the nurse inserts a syringe into the plastic tubing connected to the silver metal nozzle that has been installed directly into my vein. My heart races and beneath the tapestry of Compazine, I prepare for an assault. A cold dark whisper travels up my arm, and suddenly a chemical fragrance blooms behind my nose as I exhale, not unpleasant but unexpected, a source of sensation that is totally new. I sit ready to resist any waves of nausea, but nothing stirs in my stomach. Relief circulates through me carried by saline. I sit for thirty minutes, bathed in cool salt water, my veins washed clean, rinsed and preserved; the ordeal is over for today.

In the waiting room, my cousin sits reading. As I walk out of the chemo cell, she rises toward me, magazine in hand, concern in her eyes. "So how was it?" she asks as she embraces me. In her hair, I can see the vigorous white roots under the dark dye she uses to conceal them. This is one of the children who endured the head pounding. She has been waiting sixty years for my smile. I try to embrace her with a substitute mother's warmth. I hug her hard, and when we break the embrace, Taeko turns away quickly. I think there are tears in her eyes. For the first time, I feel gratitude that in this life, I have no children.

It is not until my cousin has driven me home and I have finished waving good-bye that the lethargy hits. Perhaps it is the Compazine, perhaps the chemotherapy chemicals. I want to lie flat with my face against the cool earth. My mother has been anxiously waiting for me to return.

"You feel like throwing up?" she asks, following me anxiously. "Take Daddy's throw up bowl." She hands me the gold, plastic, kidney-shaped receptacle that my father, who died of cancer three years ago, used to use.

"I'm fine," I say. "Can I just go to bed now? I feel so sleepy." I change out of my street clothes and into a T-shirt and slide between the sheets of my bed. My mother is anxious and I should talk with her but the need to sleep is too intense. I drift below consciousness and have the dream I used to have just after my father's death. The one where he is smiling at me so warmly that I feel enfolded and secure, the one where I go forward to embrace him then suddenly realize that he is dead. The one where I abandon him again when I tell him I cannot go with him yet.

Surgery

Operative procedure and findings:

The breast was removed from the pectoralis major with the pectoralis major muscle coming off with the breast tissue. An en bloc dissection of all auxillary tissue was then performed . . . . All other lymphoareolar and vascular tissue was excised en bloc. Specimen was sent to lab for frozen section. The area was thoroughly lavaged with saline.

With clean gloves and instruments, the wound was then closed with 4-0 Vicryl to the subcuticular tissue, closing the remaining skin with Steri-strips. Prior to that hemovac tubes were inserted. A sterile dressing was applied. The patient tolerated the procedure well . . . .

When I woke up in the hospital after the surgery three weeks ago, I couldn't tell what they had cut out. I was just relieved that they had removed the cancer. I felt pressure across my chest but no pain. I was wrapped from my armpits to my waist in gauze bandages. There were IV tubes in my arm and two large tubes coming out from beneath the bandages. Both of the tubes emerging from the white gauze were connected to a plastic squeeze bottle that was fan folded like the bellows of an accordion.

"It's a drain . . . a hemovac," the nurse explained when she came to inject snake venom called heparin into the IV tube in the back of my hand to keep the IV line unclotted and freely flowing. "That plastic bottle is squeezed until there is a vacuum. The vacuum drains the blood out of the wound so you don't get an infection." I looked apprehensively at the bright red blood collected in the plastic container. There did not seem to be a lot of blood. It seemed to be seeping out of my chest and not flowing. Each move that I made triggered a spurt of warm liquid somewhere inside the bandages, somewhere inside the tight area in my chest. Warm liquid was moving somewhere between the layers. I could not see any blood flowing beneath the white wall of bandages. I did not feel pain. Nothing spilled out into the plastic accordion-shaped bottle. The drain did not pull a matching spurt of bright, fresh blood out of my chest. It was bewildering. I could not understand what caused the sensations. Perhaps the blood in my body was confused. It used to flow smoothly from heart to muscle to breast but now it was stumbling, trying to find its new path. Perhaps it was crying in frustration. Perhaps it was strange that I was not.

Pathology Report:
The tissue subjacent to the areola contains a stony hard tumor, which covers an area measuring approximately 3 x 2.5 x 1.5 cm. Infiltrating Ductile Carcinoma.

This is typed in my medical records. Dictated by a pathologist, who probably wore a white smock covered by a black rubber apron. Who, with hands gloved and gloved again to keep out pathogens in dead tissue, probably stood over a stainless steel table looking at a portion of a human breast in a stainless steel basin. The materials of the doctor's work surface are chosen because they will absorb nothing, even the floors are probably concrete poured in a single slab so that it is able to be washed completely clean.

A breast portion in a steel basin, unconnected, an areola and epidermis which temporarily continue to cover a small mound of muscles and glands. Losing warmth, losing elasticity, draining fluid, losing color, it cannot shrink from the glare of the overhead lights as it would invariably have when it was still part of me. It can only sit in its basin, absorbing the cold of the stainless steel, contracting, drying. The areola atop it is a shameless dark brown. A bud that has never bloomed, it has never suckled a baby's hungry mouth. It used to hide dutifully in a white fiberfill bra and refuse to be caressed by any pair of teenaged hands. Now it will offer no reaction to the probing of a scalpel.

Does the doctor pause slightly to inspect the line of demarcation that runs across the skin before drawing his blade through this lump of tissue? Above the areola is a line of demarcation between contrasting hues of light and dark skin. The brown is a sunburn which was at its darkest on the day of the surgery. It is the skin's now useless memory of that day only a week ago when I, thirty-five and invulnerable, washed my car all afternoon wearing a bikini bathing suit top and a pair of jeans shorts under the bright, warm afternoon sun.

Japanese Women Don't Cry

Several days later, when the bandages finally came off I looked curiously at my chest. Where my breast used to be, there was only pale skin, which was stretched over a narrow roll of fatty tissue. Beneath that was a white scar held closed by strips of tape pressed up against my ribs. The scar looked tight and bloodless like lips pressed together maybe in fright. Below the scar, there was skin stretched taut across my rib cage and the surprise of motion. I could see the motion of my heartbeat under the skin. There used to be muscles covering my rib cage keeping the secrets deeper in my chest away from observation, but now I could suddenly see the beating of my heart. How odd the pulsating membrane of skin looked as it shuddered rhythmically. Beneath my rib cage, a drain tube emerged from a hole in my skin so matter-of-factly that only red-orange Betadine painted around it gave it fanfare. Another tube emerged from the skin of my back, which felt completely numb. The tubes met and emptied into the plastic accordion-shaped hemovac. The color of the liquid in the hemovac had by this time changed from bright red right after the surgery to a calmer more ambiguous bubblegum pink. I looked curiously at my chest; I have read stories that say that this is the point at which most women cry.

Perhaps it was those afternoons in my aunt's kitchen where she served me the previous night's Kokuho rice drenched in strong yellow tea. We ate *daikon* pickled in brine, vinegar, and sugar, and fish cooked in brown shoyu and grated ginger. She accompanied the astringent tea-soaked rice of each of these lunches with stories about Japanese women who suffered silently through a multitude of terrible things.

"When the samurai wives were captured by the enemy soldiers, they were supposed to commit *seppuku*, or hara-kiri. But death is painful and during their suffering they might struggle and fall into a position that was shameful, so before they stabbed themselves with their short swords, they would dress in white kimono, tie their legs together at the thighs, then grasp the blades of their short swords and stab themselves in the stomach, turn the short sword and cut across their abdomens, all the while not crying out." Japanese women plan ahead for every eventuality.

"When Japanese women have babies, they are silent even during the pain of childbirth. All the other women in the hospital delivery rooms are screaming but the Japanese women are silent." Anyone who would cry out cannot claim to be Japanese.

"There is a ghost story in which a good wife was poisoned by her adulterous husband. She died in agony without crying out, then came back as an *obake* and gained her revenge on the husband and his mistress." Japanese women have the right to emotional expression only after they are dead.

My aunt is a Japanese schoolteacher. She paints her face with white foundation and wears bright red lipstick. Before she draws on her eyebrows with brown pencil, she looks as if her head is made of porcelain. She reminds me of one of those life-sized puppets you see in *bunraku* with men dressed all in black hovering behind them animating them and giving them their voices.

Medical Report:
    Pt apparently doing well except for slight anorexia and still w/ post-op discomfort, sensation of pulling in left chest.

The scar runs across the left side of my chest and under my arm. The flesh under my arm and the flesh on my back feels as though it has been anesthetized with Novocain. The underside of my left arm and part of my back feel like rubber. They are no longer part of me. When I touch them with my right hand, they feel as though they belong to someone else.

My left breast and the feeling in my upper arm and the upper left back have been removed. But they are not the only things that are missing. The feeling of being safe in my own body has also disappeared. I always felt that I could run and hide if there was danger. I could curl up somewhere, small and tight, and close my eyes and stop my breathing, and the danger, growling menacingly, would scent my fear but be unable to find me, would pass me by. The danger is inside me now. "Infiltrating ductile carcinoma" means that stray cancer cells circulate in my bloodstream. Each one is able to grow and start whole colonies that can eventually kill me. I cannot run away, but I need to run to feel safe. Safety has been excised with diseased tissue. What's left is a frenzy that eats my energy.

My cousins do not visit. I think it is a protective mechanism. The healthy animals avoiding the sick. Instead, everyone in my family seems to have sent me flowers. There is a basket of lavender roses, arrangements of orchids, large cattleyas and sprays of cymbidiums in white plastic vases, yellow-and-white chrysanthemums whose petals form frilly spatters or tidy clusters, *pikake* leis, white ginger leis. Baskets and vases keep coming. They line the counters and congregate on the floors. I sit alone in my room and look at the multitude. The cumulative fragrance weighs down the air around me. I don't have to attend my funeral. I know what it will look like.

Medical Report:
    Pt started on chemotherapy last week w/ CMFVP plus Tamoxi-
fen and comes in today for her second dose of chemotherapy. Except
for slight anorexia, pt apparently doing well.

There is C which stands for *cytoxin* which can crystallize in the bladder and make patients urinate blood, the M is *methotrexate,* which is also used to treat leukemia and psoriasis and inhibits folic acid. The F stands for *fluorocil,* which sounds like a neon tube for lighting up my bones. The V drug, *vincristine*, is made from the Madagascar periwinkle, and *prednisone* is the P which will make my face swell up like the full moon in August. Last there is *Tamoxifin* which except for sterility has no side effects.

Medical Report:
    Second chemotherapy treatment. Pt reports she is going crazy.

I know I should speak more to my mother. She asks me continually how I feel. "I'm fine, fine," I tell her. Except when I mention that sounds echo in my ear, so that I feel like I am in a tunnel. Except when I drop my fork when I'm trying to eat because my fingers are getting numb, and I tell her that my shoes feel funny because my toes are also getting numb. Except when she sees the hairballs multiplying in the trash can in the bathroom. And then she asks me how I feel even more and now has taken to standing outside the bathroom door chanting an endless stream of advice while I am inside.
    "Don't drink so much Coca-Cola, see, I told you caffeine was bad for you. And you never eat any oranges so you don't have enough vitamin C.

Did you remember to drop tissue into the bowl before you go so the water doesn't splash back up on you? Did you remember to wipe yourself from front to back?"

"Ma!" I scream. "Stop it! Stop it!" And I am immediately sorry. I did not scream at her when my father was alive. I think I tried to once when I was thirteen but my father weighed in on her side and yelled at me. Since then I don't remember ever yelling at her until just now. I listen expectantly and half hope to hear my father's angry reaction. But of course, since he has been dead for three years there is nothing. "Ma, 'nough already," I say in a softer voice. She does not answer but I can hear her quick footsteps echoing down the wooden hallway. The prednisone is affecting my hearing and the sound of her footfalls seems to spiral across the walls and ceiling and echo around me. When I emerge from the bathroom, I walk into the kitchen and sit at the table. My mother looks at me sullenly but does not speak.

"We should talk about how we feel, Ma. That's what the medical social worker said," I claim with authority without apologizing. I know I should be a good daughter and apologize. I know I should stop badgering my mother. But I am driven on and on. Maybe I am getting like Big Auntie and will soon be pounding heads. My mother frowns at me and goes to the sink to wash rice for our dinner.

"Easy for you, we sent you to college so now you know how to talk, talk talk." She sniffs in irritation. There is a long pause in which the only sound is the rattling of uncooked rice grains against the aluminum sides of the pot in her hands. The metallic patter of rice grains echoes like swirling water in my ears. Then suddenly, "You cried?" She asks without turning toward me.

"About getting cancer?" I ask defensively, thinking she knows that I have so far not shed a single tear.

"No, when Daddy died. You cried?" She asks.

"Only a little at first, but six months afterward I cried when I was driving the car home. I used to cry on the highway all the time when I was driving by myself."

"I never did, you know," she reveals. "My friends say that's not good for the body. But I cannot cry. Not even once." She pauses in her rice washing and waits for my reaction.

"You should cry, Ma. That means that you're dealing with your feelings about what happened. It's not good for your health if you don't cry." I try to be sympathetic and hope that she does not sense the irony. She seems to soften at this evidence of my concern and goes on speaking.

"Daddy was different to you, you know. When I had my hysterectomy surgery, he never did take care of me. He never even would wash rice. I had to get up and cook as soon as I came back from the hospital." She inserts the rice pot in the rice cooker and comes to sit next to me at the table. "The social worker who came when Daddy was sick, she told me that at least Daddy told her he appreciated me taking care of him. But I never did cry after he died." She does not look into my eyes and ends up staring at my thinning hair instead. "He never did help me around the house. Men, they all like that, they treat the wife and the daughter different. Every time you used to get sick he used to blame me. He was really mad the time when you got pneumonia." Suddenly, I have a realization.

"Ma, this is not your fault that I got cancer. It just happened," I say.

"Of course it's my fault," she says to my surprise. "How can it not be my fault; I'm your mother."

My mother is the oldest daughter in a family of six children. I once saw a picture in a textbook captioned, *Japanese girl, 1920.* It shows an eight- or nine-year-old girl with black hair cut in bangs straight across her forehead. She is wearing a kimono and strapped to her back is an enormous baby. She is the caretaker of this helpless younger sibling. She looks like an ant struggling with a boulder. She wears an expression that is a mixture of fear, grief, and resignation. I have often wondered if it is a picture of my mother.

Mortality

When we are young, our belief in our immortality is thick and durable as denim. We can use it to fashion innumerable futures to wear over ourselves. As we grow older, the cloth of our illusion thins gently and inevitably into gossamer transparency.

This is the phone call in which I found out the results of my biopsy.

"Ms. Hayashi, your biopsy . . ."

"Yes, how bad was it?" I managed to ask through what sounded like the backwash of a jet engine roaring in my ears.

"Well, I don't know—that is to say that there was cancer and it was not cancer from the original site . . . that is, it has spread."

After a long silence, I produced what seemed to be the most logical question. "So how long do I have?"

"The thing is . . . I don't know. It may be a very long time but the point is that it is very serious. It is life threatening. I'm not the one who will deal with this. You need to see an oncologist . . . ."

"So, I'm going to die."

"Well, we are all going to die, Ms. Hayashi, and we cannot know when, but this is very serious. In terms of staging, this is beyond the first stage at this point. But as to how long, I don't know. You need to be evaluated . . . by another doctor, you see . . . soon."

"Today?"

"No . . . but within the week."

This is only the conversation. What is missing in this re-creation is the sound of a raging river of blood rushing in my ears, the roaring of thoughts, the voices urging me to run away, fly away, fly far away. Go now. Run! Run! Run away from the sound of claws tearing through safety. And the smaller voice that is too frightening to listen to. The one that growls that the danger has already invaded my body and is now part of me. I sat on the couch all through that night until the sky lightened into dawn. I sat looking longingly at a bottle full of aspirin, wondering if a whole bottle of little white tablets could become a ticket into oblivion. Japanese women don't cry out in childbirth; they bind their legs together so that they do not fall into a shameful position during suicide. They stare dry-eyed for twelve hours at the possibility of a botched suicide attempt. I sat until the next morning; then, with my belief in immortality and my future shredded into strips around me, I picked up the telephone to make an appointment to see the oncologist.

I remember the moment that my mother discovered her own mortality. My mother is putting up the hem on the dress I will wear to my first day in the sixth grade. I make my own clothes but my mother hems them better than I do. She sews with invisible stitches, blind stitches, she calls them. She learned them and drafting, that is, creating her own patterns, at sewing school when she was a girl.

"You lucky," she says to me as I sit on the floor where I am laying out the jigsaw puzzle pieces of tissue-paper patterns over the long piece of fabric that stretches from the front door to the end of the living room. "You can go to the store and buy the patterns you want nowadays. We had to make our own." My mother frowns as she re-threads her needle. She cuts a new length of thread, moistens one end of the strand in her mouth, then twirls the filaments in the thread together tightly. Holding the thread in one hand and the needle with the other, she attempts to put the end of the thread through the tiny steel eye of the needle. She holds the needle closer to her face then farther away. Blinking in irritation, she removes her bifocals and tries again.

"Getting old . . ." she sighs.

"How old are you, Mommy?" I ask from my seat on the smooth wood floor at the other end of the living room. My mother puts down the needle then thinks out loud and recites the story I have heard many times before.

"You were born when I was thirty-three years old . . . now you are eleven . . . so I'm forty-four. I'm an old lady," she sighs.

"You're not old yet, Mommy. How old was Obachan when she died?" I ask.

"My mother died when she was sixty-nine," my mother muses. "That means I'll be sixty-nine in . . ." she pauses, calculating "in twenty-five years!" She exclaims. Then she turns suddenly, her face breaking. "I have only twenty-five years left to live . . . ." Twenty-five years. She had married at twenty-seven, she had been married seventeen years, it must suddenly have seemed like the blink of an eye. The stitches unraveling in her lap, her eyes taking me in, she realizes she will abandon me when I am only thirty-six, younger than the age at which her own mother had gone away from her. She wipes her cheeks and turns away from me then stands hurriedly and scurries along the river of fabric that covers the living room floor toward the bathroom at the back of our cottage. Her heels leave little round wrinkled prints on the tissue paper pattern pieces. I can see drops of water where her tears soak into and soften the tissue. Ever since that time, I have often wondered when I would have this same moment of discovery. Until now, I have never envied her that moment.

Other Women with Cancer

Saleswomen stare at the wispy strands of my hair and my scalp, which is daily becoming more assertive, but say nothing. I begin wearing brightly colored scarves to hide my condition. But now in the waiting room of the oncologist's office each week, I am becoming more and more visible. Several old ladies with scarves covering their hair, who have ignored me for the last month, begin to look at me with interest.

"You picking up your grandma?" asks the little 4' 10" woman in the green dress, whose wig is too large and whose lipstick is too red.

"No, I'm going for chemotherapy," I answer. The tiny woman comes to sit next to me, smiles mischievously.

"You going for chemo? What kind of cancer you get?" I am interesting to her. She stares intently into my eyes, her mouth turned up into a grin.

"I have breast cancer," I whisper. She puts a wiry hand on mine. The red, red nail polish on each of her fingers gleams above her cool, smooth caress. Neither of us is insulated by any illusions and I can feel her vibrant touch against my naked skin.

"Only breast cancer," she says, "I get liver cancer . . . over three years." She pauses and chortles, "And I went to Las Vegas four times between the chemo, you know." She smiles a kiss at me as the nurses call her in for her treatment.

The next week, there is the woman who has multiple swellings on the left side of her skull, who struggles to navigate the walkway up to the oncologist's office. She lists to one side, then stumbles toward the railing. I run forward to catch her.

"Why, thank you," she murmurs graciously, and I look past the swellings on her skull and directly into her eyes. I am startled that they are still beautiful. She looks at the scarves covering my hair and at the Band-Aid on the back of my hand, which covers the newest perforation in the green vein that runs across it. She straightens up, then caresses my arm.

"You know, I've had this cancer over fourteen years. It started as breast cancer then came back and I fought it down," she tells me as she steadies herself. "I had two children to raise, you see. And I raised them. But now, well now, I need a little help sometimes." She smiles as she leans into me. I lean back gently, just enough to steady her as I walk her into the oncologist's office.

Then today, there is the tall woman who enters the elevator outside the lab the same time that I do. We both hold our arms bent upward, pressing on the small white squares of gauze taped over the fresh puncture wounds left by the hollow hypodermic needles used to draw blood. She wears a plain cotton dress, which looks as if she made it herself. She moves stiffly, as if favoring her left side. She looks apprehensively around the elevator and her eyes come to rest on me. I smile slightly, but it is enough.

"Can you tell me the way to Dr. Ho's office?" she asks hesitantly. Dr. Ho is my oncologist. I look at her face, which is ordinary and unadorned by any cosmetics. She would be plain except for her hair, which is long and swept up into a French braid and pinned neatly to the back of her head.

"Yes, you get off on the ground floor and follow the signs to the Palma building," I instruct her. She manages to look grateful even though it is clear that she is still anxious. I punch the button for the first floor and hold the door open for her as she smiles nervously and begins walking in the direction I have indicated for her. Her hair is the color of red garnets and wisps that have escaped the hairpins glow softly in the afternoon sun. I watch her walk down the concrete pathway to the oncologist's office, and I cannot make myself leave the elevator to join her. The elevator doors close on me, and I find I must ride up to the top floor and back down again before I can see well enough to press any buttons. I cannot make out the numbers through my tears.

The House

Sam sat on the kitchen floor leaning against the refrigerator, feeling the current of warm air from under the humming machine swirl over her legs. She liked the contrast, the cold clean linoleum and the warmth of the air that flowed from beneath the white metal box.

The water and wax had just dried leaving the floor beautifully cool and she lay down to feel the contrast of warm and cool over a larger area of her skin. She had just washed and waxed the floor using dishcloths. An old boyfriend had once told her that his grandmother cleaned their kitchen floor that way and she'd done it on her hands and knees the same way ever since. That was several boyfriends ago. She was married to Bobby now, and they had just bought this large house. In the quiet of the new house, the protective humming of the refrigerator settled on the cool kitchen floor, pushed outward over the olive-green carpet and continued until it filled the unoccupied rooms. It was a good house and she was proud they owned it. They were only in their thirties. They were the first of their friends to own a house. The house was far outside of the city.

"Makakilo," her aunt had said. "Who will drive all the way out there from Honolulu?" Perhaps that was why she had convinced her husband to buy it. It was on a hill and in the morning and evening, she could stand outside on the lanai and look out at the *kiawe* trees and the ocean beyond. Some mornings there was mist closing her in so that her house, filled with warm humming, became a capsule, a womb, floating.

Today she would be alone in her kitchen until nine at night. Her husband was going straight to the driving range after work. She'd made a pot of stew yesterday and stuck it in the refrigerator so she had nothing to do until he came home. She would wait until he came home to eat her own dinner. It was not something she liked to do; waiting so long to eat made her nibble on junk food during the early evening. But she liked to have the food hot and ready for him. Early in their marriage, she had asked him how the food tasted hoping to please him.

"Okay," was all he ever said.

"But did you like the seasonings? Did you like what I did with the garnish? How did it taste?" she would press him. He would look puzzled and uncomfortable.

"It was okay, I ate it . . . ." he'd answer, then turn his head and stare intently at whatever appeared on the screen of the television set he kept in the dining room. She had tried asking again, but he would turn his body away from her and let the television's light bathe him fully so that all she could see of his eyes was the violence and color reflected on his glasses from the screen. It was in those early days that she had hit upon the rating system.

"Was it a 10?" she'd ask. "Was the dinner a 10?"

"Well, maybe it was an 8," he'd say. "If we had miso soup and dessert, it would have been a 10." She asked him automatically now whenever he ate. It was not that he would ever complain about food. Once when she had to go out, he volunteered to make his own dinner. She'd come home to find him eating Wheaties and watching television.

We have a house, she'd enumerate to herself. We have two cars. We have two master's degrees. Our combined income is more than my father ever made. She dusted her koa wood dining set. She used the same bottled furniture polish that the piano salesman had recommended her mother use when her parents had bought her a piano when she was ten. It was getting dark and she still had so much time before she needed to reheat the stew for dinner. Dusk always made her feel an empty sadness she could never explain. She went back to the kitchen and was about to pick up the phone with the extra long cord.

The phone rang.

"Hello?"

"Hey, Sam," said a cheery voice. It was her friend Sarah. "I had to talk to someone; the kids are driving me crazy." Sarah had three growing boys. She was married to an engineer. She and Sam had gone to intermediate school together.

"What you doing?" Sarah asked.

"Cleaning . . ." Sam answered.

"I wish I had time to clean. Brian is driving me nuts. I had to buy a harness to put on that kid. Now when people see us in the mall they make side-eye at me and say, 'I treat my *dog* betta than that.' They can say what they like, they not going pay my doctor bills. Last week in the store, that kid disappeared while I was writing my check, and the next thing I know, he's coming out from under a clothes rack covered with blood."

"Wow." Sam felt the tiny ache in her stomach. She and Bobby had no children and she'd had a couple of mini-surgeries where the doctor cut a hole in her navel to insert a scope.

"So, how's things?" Sarah asked.

"Oh, still no luck," Sam replied. Sarah had not explicitly asked the question, but they both knew what the conversation was about.

"Be happy and enjoy the peace and quiet!" Sarah was a nurse. She had struggled through nursing school, married soon after graduation, and was raising her family when everyone else was still in graduate school and beginning new careers. "I'm baking a cake for Bible study group; I can't do anything tomorrow because there's soccer. Then we have to go to the temple for my father's three-year memorial service." Sarah paused. "Nuts yeah? Go to Bible study and then go to the Buddhist temple for the three-year service?" Sam felt the sadness again. She brushed it aside.

"Three years since your father died? Fast . . ." Sam said.

"Yeah, but I still feel the pain like it was only yesterday." Sarah was forthright and open as the sky on a tradewind day. "You know, I'm a nurse and I should have listened to him when he said he had pain. But the kids and Dennis, yeah? We were doing so much. Plus, my father never complained very much . . ." Sarah paused.

"But it wasn't your fault, he was in his nineties," Sam hurried to add. "Even the doctors didn't know he had an obstruction." She thought of her own father. He had been dead only six months. She was still getting up at four each morning in response to a dream in which she thought she heard his voice calling her. She did not tell Sarah this. She had never told anyone.

"Hey!" A loud crash echoed in the earpiece along with childish laughter. "You guys better be in that bathtub when Mommy gets off this phone!" Sarah yelled toward the laughter. "Bye, Sam, gotta go."

Sam dangled the telephone receiver by its cord tail and watched as it spun frantically, untwisting itself. Then she hung up and walked upstairs through the quiet house to the small bathroom. She loved the house; it was quiet and orderly. Her husband was like that. It was why she married him. Her mother's house was always a mess. There were things piled on top of things on every flat surface.

"You that's why," her mother always said. "You always so messy." She had believed it too. Because it had always been that way and she had never had any cause to doubt it. After she'd gotten a job and been assigned to her own classroom, she had noticed that her classroom generally stayed neat. Her room in the teachers' cottage had also always been neat. It had been only then that she had begun to suspect that her mother might be the one who was really the mess maker.

She undressed and got into the tub in the small bathroom. The house had two full baths, but she preferred her own bathtub to the one her husband used. This was illogical. Using two bathrooms meant that she had to clean two bathrooms. But Bobby was so . . . he never said anything about her using his bathroom, but she'd watched him take a piece of toilet tissue and carefully wipe her hair off the artificial marble counters and carefully pick the long black strands out of the bathtub before he got in. It was just part of his personality. He once grumbled at her for using a pencil from his desk.

"But I used it yesterday." She had been exasperated. "How did you even know I went in there and used your pencil? I put it back."

"Yes, but you put it back wrong," he had said quietly. "I always put pencils back in the box with their points facing one way. That way only one side of the box has pencil scratches on it and the other side stays clean." He looked sullen as he erased the marks she had made on the box he kept his pencils in.

Sam could imagine what Sarah might say about her husband. But the five years they had been married had been the most orderly ones she had spent in her life. After living in her mother's house, she valued the serenity of clean tabletops and long empty expanses of counter space that you didn't have to walk by carefully. She'd often gotten blamed when as a child she'd touched the wrong thing on the overloaded countertop and everything fell off. She had been able for the first time in her life to have people over for parties. Her husband organized her kitchen for her once a year. She actually enjoyed cleaning things up and putting things back into their places.

"My life is actually perfect now." She sighed to herself as she slipped into the bath. She pinched the backs of her hands. The skin settled quickly back into place. She had been doing this pinch for most of her life. She'd learned it from her grandmother.

"Pinch Baba's skin," the old woman would say as she held her three-year-old grandchild in her lap. Sam remembered the brown blotchy skin was cool and leathery. She carefully picked a flat spot between the blue green veins. Her little fingers pinched the skin and they both watched the ridge she created in the back of her grandmother's hand. It took a long time for the skin to finally flatten out and settle back again. Sam was fascinated. Her grandmother would laugh.

"That's how you can tell you're old." Her grandmother said in Kumamoto-ken, rough-as-a-scrub-brush Japanese. "When your skin comes like Baba's, then you can tell you're old."

Maybe Bobby had his own pinch test, Sam thought as she settled into the warm water. He had been saying things lately. "We're both thirty already. We really should have a family; otherwise, what are we living for? It's selfish for us to have all this only for ourselves." She would have liked to answer that she was truly content. She would have liked to say that if they could just talk things over once in a while, maybe he would understand. But she never did.

"I told you I wanted chocolate mocha ice cream for dessert," she remembered saying to him last week as he came back to the car carrying two cups of pineapple sherbet.

"Yeah, but I knew you'd like this better," he'd said. "And if you don't want it, I can have two desserts." It was no use saying anything; he was just like that. She got out of the tub and dried herself as the water drained away.

She heard the car pull into the carport. Bobby would be in the house soon so she hurried to get her clothes on. She slipped on one of her father's old T-shirts over a pair of shorts. She liked the familiar smell.

"Hi, Sweetie, what's for dinner?" he said as he entered the door.

"Stew and rice down in the kitchen," she called as she went down the stairs to prepare their plates. Bobby went straight to the downstairs bedroom to unload his things. She had once been at her friend Maria's house when Maria's husband came home. She had been surprised that Maria dropped everything to rush to the door and greet him. She had even been embarrassed to see them kiss each other lightly on the lips. Her mother and father had never made a big thing of each other's homecomings.

"It's going to take me about fifteen minutes to warm up the stew," she called to him from the kitchen. There was no answer. "It's going to take me about fifteen minutes to get the stew ready," she repeated loudly. There was only the refrigerator's humming. Sam turned on the stove and lifted the cover off the pot of stew. She added frozen green peas and closed the lid. Sometimes she wished Bobby would come into the kitchen just to watch her cook. He never had in all the years they had been married. Recently, she had watched a movie on the Japanese channel on television. The story was about a Japanese housewife who was convinced that she had become invisible. Her husband came in the door, went to the bedroom to change, and then came to the dining room table to be fed. He never noticed his wife or spoke to her. She'd tried serving him unusual dishes; she'd tried wearing outrageous outfits; she'd even gotten her sister to play her part as housewife one day and he never noticed. Sam lifted the lid of the rice cooker and wrapped a dishtowel around it. She then stirred the white grains with the wooden *shakushi* and put the cover back down over the rice. Her aunt who was born in Japan had always done it that way.

"Hi, Sweetie," Bobby called from the dining room. Sam was about to answer when she heard the sound of the television news. He had already turned on the set without waiting for her answer. Sam went to the refrigerator and got out a cucumber for a salad. She washed it then cut a tiny slice off the tip. She took the slice and rubbed it back and forth over the end of the cucumber until white foam emerged from the cucumber. Then she threw away the little slice and washed the whole cucumber under running water, before cutting the vegetable into thin slices. She didn't know why she did this. Her mother, her aunt, every Japanese woman she had ever seen making a salad did this same thing to cucumbers and even zucchinis, before slicing them up. When she asked them why, they always said the same words, "*aku wo dasu*," which meant, "removes the bitterness." She arranged the cucumber slices on a plate. She scooped rice into a bowl, then ladled stew on top of it. She carried Bobby's bowl of stew out into the dining room and set it on the table in front of him. He was reading an investment newsletter and listening to the television news. He did not look up at her. She tried to remember the ending of the Japanese movie about the invisible housewife but she could not.

"How would you describe yourselves as a family?" the motherly looking social worker was asking.

"Just normal, I guess." Sam fidgeted with her shoe, slipping it on and off her heel. The Family Services office was bright and cheerful looking. She had to come here today for a pre-adoption interview. They had been trying to have a baby for the last five years and now they were applying for adoption.

"Covering all bases," Bobby had said.

"So, tell me, dear, how do you feel about adoption?" The social worker was writing things down on a yellow legal pad. Sam was glad that the social worker was an Oriental woman. She never looked directly into Sam's eyes while they talked.

"Well," Sam started. Her ideal baby appeared before her. It was a boy with her father's eyes and dimpled smile. She'd missed that smile in the last six months since he died. Then emptiness welled up and Sam could no longer see the baby's face. "I've been trying to have a baby for the last five years," she began. "I've gone for lots of tests and laparoscopies, you know, where they cut a hole in your navel and look in." They had been trying to have a baby for so long. Her mother and father had wanted to have grandchildren. She was an only child, no brothers or sisters to take over and deliver a little one. Sam looked at the filaments in the gray carpet; there were thousands of them. It must be comforting to be one of a thousand instead of an only one.

"So, dear, you haven't been successful so far? Why don't you go on trying?" The social worker startled her. She was leaning in Sam's direction and looking at her intently. Sam frowned and then smiled lamely to cover it. Her father was dead. She'd run out of time. That wasn't exactly true. In her mind, she saw the wrinkled purple scar on her mother's abdomen. She had refused the exploratory surgery that her mother and cousin had had.

"I just couldn't," Sam said before realizing it. "I mean, we're already in our mid-thirties. If we don't keep all of our options open . . . I mean, my husband says we aren't getting any younger. My parents always wanted grandchildren and they're already dead." Sam was playing with her fingers and tapping her foot.

"Yes, but what do *you* want?" The social worker stared straight into her eyes.

"My mother said from the time I was little, I had baby dolls and I carried my baby cousin around a lot." Sam crossed her arms in front of her body. She hated these questions. She hated any conversation that included the words *be you, be yourself.* She felt that she was floating in the air over a vast pit. The bottom of the pit was gray like the carpet.

"Well, I think I have what I need, dear," the social worker said with a small note of hesitation in her voice. "We'll schedule the home visits for next week, then." Sam didn't know whether to be relieved or not. Had she passed? Everyone told them the process would take a long, long time.

In the dream, it was always the same. She floated along on the black inner tube. The sun was shining. Her hair and shoulders and arms felt warm as the sun beat down on them. The surface of the fat inner tube was hot and coated with a film of white salt crystals from the water. She could see the sand of the beach, which was the color of freshly grated coconut. Beyond the sand, she could see the green mountains holding up the blue sky. The black rubber surface of the inner tube absorbed the heat of the sun and began to burn her skin. She slipped down into the water to cool off. Her hands couldn't hold on to the smooth rubber, and soon the inner tube bobbed away. She couldn't touch bottom. She had floated out too far. She grabbed for the inner tube. It was too wide, and she couldn't grasp it. It kept receding from her on the water. She went under, and the world became gray-green water, which pressed in on her. She felt her heart beating wildly. She felt the water turn cold as ice. Then two strong hands grabbed her. She felt the rescuing warmth of his hands against her skin in the cold water.

"Daddy!" she called out. She opened her eyes. Bobby was asleep beside her on the bed. There was no one else in the bedroom. No one else was in the house.

She missed her father. She could not think of him without thinking of the ocean. One of her last memories of him was walking along Sandy Beach with him looking for shards of beach glass. He was, by that time, in his sixties, and the color in his hair and even the irises of his eyes had been bleached by the sea and the sun. His skin was a rich dark brown, the color of strong coffee, the color of his undiluted acceptance of himself and of her because she was his daughter. They walked with eyes downcast, searching the sand; she walked ahead, he, behind her, always parallel to the surf.

"Never turn your back to the sea. Waves come in sets, the ones you see breaking now are not the largest, not the smallest. The ocean is always changing; never take your eyes off it." It was a truth a fisherman's daughter learned early; it was one of the first things she had been taught. She walked ahead of him quickly. Her mind was always distracted as she walked, thinking of some slight, some worry, jumping from one point to another. He had always laughingly compared her to a small fish, darting, quick, changing direction. He walked slowly, surely through the sand behind her. His mind quiet, eyes with faded irises searching. He always found them first, hidden under sand that she had already passed over. Green, brown, white, translucent, nickel-sized pieces of broken glass ground smooth and benevolent by the pounding of the surf. He had had years of searching in sandy bottoms for *tako* holes to hone his skill.

"Too good ah your fadda?" He'd say as he handed her another gem to add to the growing hoard in her pockets. When they had walked together for more than an hour, and every one of her pockets was bulging, they would sit together on a sand dune facing the ocean and listen to the waves breaking. It sounded like the earth itself softly inhaling and exhaling.

He would look out over the ocean, into the translucent waves. "You know, I used to sit by my mother when she was dying. I used to listen to her breathing, which was the only sound she could make after her stroke. I used to sit and listen to her for hours." He stared out over the gently rising and falling blue surface. His irises were white rimmed and his hair almost pure white. "She sent you, you know. We didn't have a baby long time and we thought, mo betta go spend all our money and go around the world. Afta my mother died, we traveled as far as Hilo. When we came home, your mother was *hapai*. That was because of your grandma, she sent you." He handed her this story as he had handed her the beach glass gems.

"Why didn't you adopt?" she asked.

"No adopt," he said turning away from her. She thought of the jagged knotted scar across her mother's abdomen. Her mother had been cut open by doctors doing exploratory surgery so that things could be put right with her womb. Sam knew that unlike her mother, she had refused the exploratory surgery. Even if Grandma did send her a baby with her father's special eyes, her body would have no place to put it.

Now he was gone, and the longing to replace him bloomed in her soul and lingered as insistently as the fragrance of *pikake* blossoms. He could see things, find the treasures for her. If she had had a hard time with Bobby, she would go to her father and his calm eyes would soon find some blessing she had missed seeing in her life that day. She could sit talking to him while he remembered that when she was a child with bangs cut straight across her forehead, she chattered like a mynah bird and she drank water like a little fish. She knew how proud he was that she, the child of a high school dropout, had finished college. She collected his stories until the bottomless pocket that was her soul was filled again, and she could go home happy.

Since he died, there were more and more gray ocean dreams. She slipped off the inner tube into the cold ocean. There were no warm arms to catch her. She would wake in bed and find only Bobby asleep on the sheets beside her. Desperately, she would count the things she still had like colored glass pebbles worn smooth in her hands, her job where she felt real, her house with its clean countertops and deep green rug. She counted them to anchor herself in warmth. Still, there was the fear she felt that one day she would not wake up after she had gone under. She felt that one day, instead of waking up, she would disappear.

The baby appeared unexpectedly. The social worker said that he was the son of a Japanese student and a married local man. Marriage was out of the question for the couple, and the birth mother felt she could not return to Japan with a fatherless infant. Sam remembered the phone call; the social worker would appear at her door with the child at two that afternoon. She felt panic, fear that she would do something stupid, and the overwhelming fear that she would be so incompetent that she would harm the baby.

She picked up the phone to call Bobby. He was too busy at his job. He could not come home until later in the day. She would have to handle it alone. The child arrived wrapped in a blue blanket. He was wearing a blue bonnet. He had a tiny blue T-shirt on over a blue diaper and blue knit shoes.

The social worker beamed as she thrust the infant into Sam's arms. Sam held him and looked down at his face. She felt the softness of the blue blanket, the warmth of his body, looked into the beauty of his tiny face, and felt nothing, no rush of warmth, no maternal feeling, no tears of joy. She felt only fear.

"Take it easy," said Sarah over the phone. "Lots of mothers don't automatically bond with their babies. You should have seen me. There I was after twelve hours of labor and I heard the third one cry. You don't know how much I wanted a girl. The nurses all didn't want to look at me. 'Is it a girl?' I wanted to know but I couldn't even ask. Then I knew—because all the nurses kept saying, 'Beautiful baby! Congratulations, Mrs. Nakamura!' I knew that after the nine months and all that pain in labor that it was another boy!"

Sam's mind was consumed with a mad rush to get things—trapped, panic, the baby had to eat, she had to get bottles; he came with a backpack, one bottle, one can of powdered formula. Bobby wouldn't come home. Sam couldn't move. The baby needed a car seat, a crib, clothes, blankets, diapers, more bottles, brushes, bathtub, so many things, a myriad of things. All at once. Adding water to the canned powder instantly produced milk to nourish. Shake the bottle; avoid caking the powder in the nipple. What was caked in her soul?

She watched the milk flow into his tiny rosebud mouth. Why was nothing flowing from her heart?

Bath, don't cry, don't cry. Undress him, no, first run the water, no, first scrub down the basin. But where to put the baby while she worked? If she put him down he would cry. Can't scrub the basin with him in her arms. Wait until he goes to sleep, make sure he's asleep then scrub the basin.

When Bobby finally arrived home at five, Sam dropped the baby in his arms, promised to be back as soon as possible. "His formula's made and in the icebox," she'd yelled as she sprinted for the garage. "Supposed to warm the bottle in warm water, not the microwave…test it before you feed him."

She drove as fast as she could for Pearlridge. She bought bottles, powdered milk, diapers, blankets, baby clothes, bottlebrushes, car seat, almost forgot the car seat. Bobby was in the house with a baby; she couldn't leave him for long.

After the dishes were washed, the kitchen counters sanitized, the eight bottles boiled, the powdered formula measured, the eight nipples and collars reassembled and ready for the next day, after she had checked on the baby's position again, she slipped outside and sat under the fleshy leaves of the neighbor's stephanotis vine leaning lazily on their chain-link fence. She felt the heat of the gravel of the driveway under her thighs and waited for some maternal feeling to rise in her soul. There was only cold gray where her heart should have been. She sobbed. For her father who would never return, for the baby that her grandmother would never send, for the baby safely asleep in its crib that she felt no connection to. For the human life that she was not a part of. Her tears were tiny drops of salty water. Tiny and inadequate substitutes for the ocean of love that she and her father had so effortlessly shared.

The nights were short and dreamless. She always woke in the darkness to the baby's cries before she had time to dream. The days were divided into intervals. The pediatrician had told her never to overfeed the child. "He must eat all his formula at one sitting so that he will sleep soundly before the next feeding. If he takes only a little formula at one feeding, resist giving him the bottle again until he is due for the next feeding. It's okay if he's a little hungry in between. It's okay for him to cry."

She fed the baby at six. He took only half the bottle then played for an hour. He then got hungry again and wanted the bottle. Sam had to resist feeding him until ten. He got restless and fussy and began to cry when his stomach was empty. She walked with him, she rocked him, she turned on his tinkling toys. None of them satisfied him. He wanted his bottle. He whimpered miserably for the next hour and a half before falling into a restless sleep.

She called the doctor and said, "I need to feed him."

"Don't spoil him," the doctor lectured her. "Mothers who give in and are controlled by their babies raise fat toddlers and obese adults," he insisted.

"What I going do?" she asked Bobby. "I can't feed him when he wants to eat, he's unhappy, I'm no good at this." Bobby made no reply as he played on a blanket on the floor with the baby. He would come home after work and play with the baby for an hour while Sam worked in the kitchen to get dinner on the table. After dinner, Bobby, looking preoccupied, would disappear into his office, leaving Sam alone with the infant again.

"There's something wrong," she told the social worker. The woman nodded sagely.

"You feel like you're baby-sitting?" she asked.

"Yes," Sam answered into her lap. How shameful it was. Only monsters couldn't love their babies. "What's wrong with me? The baby is beautiful. I should be grateful. Anyone would find it easy to love him."

"Calm down," the older woman answered. "These things take time, sometimes months. Then suddenly, something happens and you realize that you are his mother. Or sometimes," the woman shifted slightly, "women never bond completely with their babies. Sometimes, it is the father, not the mother, who establishes the bond with the infant, sometimes, the grandmother. Life is not perfect, you know . . . ." The social worker looked at Sam and smiled. "But I think you are one of those women who will bond in time." Sam sighed, looked down at the infant in her arms and willed herself to agree.

But time evaporated the next evening. "I've been transferred to the office in Ohio," Bobby came home and announced. "My new boss wants his friend to manage the Honolulu office," he added angrily. "I don't know what that guy wants. He just gives me projects and tells me to get them done. I ask him to tell me exactly how and he just says, 'Use your own judgment.' I guess this means he didn't like my judgment," Bobby finished bitterly.

"Doesn't he know that we're adopting a baby?" Sam asked, aware that the spit-up milk covering the left shoulder of her blouse gave off a rancid smell.

"His friend is coming into town next week. They need to have the Ohio office covered," Bobby said. "I have to leave in a couple of days. I'll look for a house for us there. I'll call you every day." Sam felt herself floating. They had lived on the mainland before. The gray mornings, the smoggy air, the water from the tap that she could not drink. The strange black and white people striding around in overcoats. People who offered to save her soul in the Kmart parking lot, people who complimented her on her ability to speak English. She had not known how to do anything. She did not know how to dress, polyester print blouses and double-knit pants over pantyhose did not keep out the cold. She had gone out to the car one frosty morning and found her key did not open the lock. She went back into the house and came out with warm water to throw on the lock. Bobby stopped her before she realized that that would have turned the door into a solid block of ice.

"I don't want to go back there" was all he heard her say as he headed to his office. She remembered feeling poisoned the last time they had lived on the mainland. *Aku wo dasu*, she wished there was a ritual like cutting the tip off a cucumber and rubbing it back and forth to draw out the foamy bitterness that had built up in her soul.

She called the social worker the next day. "You have to adopt the baby before you can leave the state." The woman was very firm. "You have to make the decision irrevocable."

"But I'm not sure yet," was all Sam could whisper.

A team of social workers arrived to meet with Sam and Bobby. After a few minutes of listening to their comments, Sam realized that her usual social worker was an advocate for her; another worker, a man, was an advocate for Bobby; and a third woman was an advocate for the baby.

"We can expedite the paperwork so that you can take the baby with you when you leave," the male worker explained. "We have the forms here and if you sign now we can begin the process." He turned to Bobby.

"Yeah, we'll sign now," Bobby said. Sam sat silently. Thoughts tumbled in her head like sand and seaweed caught in a rip current.

I don't know if I am his mother. What if we adopt him and I never feel like his mother? What if he gets to be a teenager and he knows that I don't feel one hundred percent love for him? He'll know. I can't lie to him. The turbulence in her head disoriented her.

"What do you say, dear?" Sam's usual social worker asked. Sam, startled out of the churning jumble of her thoughts, looked around from face to face.

"Of course we'll sign," Bobby repeated. Sam was startled to realize that she had never gone against his opinion in five years of marriage. She was like the woman in the Japanese television show. She was not sure if Bobby saw her anymore. What if she signed and she never felt that the baby was one hundred percent hers? Maybe she could raise the baby even though she wasn't sure. Maybe it was enough that Bobby and the baby belonged to one another. She argued furiously with herself. Of course the baby would know. What child would not know? What child could be raised by an expanse of cold, gray ocean? But what would Bobby do if she disagreed with him?

"But I don't know if I am his mother yet," she protested softly. Bobby looked irritated.

"She's going to be his mother and I'm going to be his father. That's the way it is," Bobby said. He sounded as though he was writing a play and she was a character in it. "Look, if I don't leave for Ohio next week, I'm going be fired; we can't raise a child if I don't have a job. We'll just do it and that's it," he concluded.

"But I don't know," Sam whispered softly, holding on to the couch cushions. She pictured the flat, gray countryside, with gray skies. The social workers looked very concerned at this impasse that had developed. The motherly social worker spoke first.

"Well, you need to be absolutely certain, dear," she said encouragingly. "Perhaps Bobby could ask his boss to delay his transfer until you feel more confident about your feelings."

"I told you, my boss is unreasonable." Bobby insisted. "He just got transferred in here and he wants his friends around him. I have to leave."

"There is a solution," the male social worker spoke up. "Bobby may adopt the child on his own, that would be perfectly acceptable," he pointed out.

"No, she is the wife and has to raise the baby. I am the husband and I have to work," insisted Bobby, by this time exasperated. "I cannot take care of a baby and set up a new office in Ohio; she has to come up to take care of the baby." Sam looked at their faces in turn; she had never seen Bobby so animated. It seemed as though he was trying to save his version of their life.

"But I don't know if I'm attached to him yet. What if, what if I never get attached to him?" was all she could think of to say. The social worker that had been silent up until now then spoke.

"The baby has only a little more time left before he recognizes the adults in his life. In perhaps two to three weeks, he will begin to make attachments. You must decide now if he is to stay with you, or if you want to give him a chance to go to a new home."

"Will he be hurt if I give him up now?" Sam asked fearfully.

"No, from what we know about child development, he has not yet made strong attachments. At this point, as long as he is fed, bathed, held, and talked to, he is developing normally. If you hold on too long and give him up in the next month, or the next, I think the possibility of harm is very real. You must make up your mind soon."

"If I give him up, will I be able to adopt a baby again?" Sam asked slowly. She was amazed at the answer.

"Yes, it is very possible that you will be able to adopt at another time in your life, especially if you can show that your circumstances have changed," was the motherly social worker's reassuring answer.

The male social worker closed his portfolio and ended the session by saying, "These people have a lot to talk over together."

The motherly social worker was kindly and reassuring as she said, "Take your time, dear. Talk things over. You must do what is right for you, for Bobby, and for the baby. Call me anytime."

It was the baby's social worker who seemed most agitated. "Remember, you have only a few more days to decide. He will begin to recognize you and bond irrevocably to you soon. You will damage him if you wait too long."

There was no one to call for advice. No one she had ever known had given up a baby. Or maybe someone had, but she could not remember anyone ever speaking about it. She tried to talk with Bobby after the social workers had gone.

"If you give him up, we are no longer married," he said. Then he returned to packing.

Sam and the baby were alone in the house after Bobby left. She had succeeded in putting the baby on a schedule. He was sleeping through the night. He got up in the morning at six and she fed him his first bottle. She burped him and played with him after he ate. She put him down on a soft flannel blanket spread over the fluffy green rug and watched as he experimented with rolling over. He succeeded once when he stretched his arms up over his head.

He rolled three times before he stopped and blinked at her in surprise. She was proud that he was progressing physically, that he was gaining weight, that he seemed to be a healthy baby. Every morning, she willed herself to love him. Every morning, she had to admit that though he was beautiful, she could somehow not give her heart to him. Her heart was filling with more fear every day. Time was running out. The baby's social worker called her daily and asked if she had made a decision yet. Every day she had to admit that she could not.

Every night, she sat under the stephanotis vine after the child was asleep. She thought of her father and the unquestioning bond that they had shared. She knew that the baby deserved to have that bond with someone.

As the van receded, she turned her back and it hit her like a tsunami. She knew she was connected to the baby. The sobs broke like waves over her body. Some were small, others larger, and the largest bowled her over as they washed over her and left her drenched and gasping. She called the social worker's house. The woman was cold, business-like. "You have made your decision. Give him a chance to begin his life now." It was like trying to hold on to the water of a receding wave.

She called twenty times that day. There was no answer. She called thirty times the next day. She called the third day and was told of his next placement. "He went to a woman who had a child taken away by a birth mother who changed her mind. The social worker said that his new mother had accepted him immediately. After twelve hours, his new mother had said, 'Of course, this one has always been my baby all along. We were just waiting for each other. Now we are together as we were meant to be.'" The waves raging in her heart began to break with less force. The largest ones no longer toppled her over into sobbing, the smallest ones caused no salt water to cascade down her cheeks. She embraced herself, encircled herself with her own arms.

The moving men came the next day to pack up the household goods for shipment to Bobby's new job site. They did not ask her about the empty crib or the room full of baby things. They packed and packed until she was left with just the camping equipment and a few personal belongings she had thrown into the off-limits closet. She made herself a dinner of soup in the one pot that she had left. She ate it surrounded by the clean green carpet.

The phone rang and rang and she refused to answer it. She knew it was Bobby calling long distance. She let it ring. She slept soundly and, for the first time in four weeks, she dreamed. It was four in the morning; she awoke to the sound of her father calling her name. He was surrounded by warm radiance. She walked toward his smile. Suddenly she was aware of the pain in her heart. She remembered that she had given up the baby. She remembered that her father was dead. She pushed herself away from the bright warmth that surrounded her father like a shroud. She told him she could not go with him.

The next evening, after a day of scrubbing, cleaning, and shining the empty house, she decided to spend the night next to the refrigerator in the kitchen. She rolled the sleeping bag out next to it. The busy hum of its great white belly and the warm air blowing out from beneath it comforted her. She cried herself to sleep, curling up next to its bulk. The morning dawned, clear and golden through the curtainless window. She was strangely calm, like the glassy sea on a windless day. She remembered that there had been a new dream. A little girl with bangs cut straight across her forehead showed her a pocketful of beach glass. The child touched her cheek and said, "Don't worry, I'm coming." She remembered the calming warmth of the small child's embrace. "Don't worry, I'm almost here."

To Flo

I have a terrible time
between your death and burial.
My head pounds,
but tears refuse to fall.
At forty-five you've gone.
A heart attack, they say uncertainly.
Lynn and I
go now to visit your husband and sons.
We carry purple chrysanthemums and
dark green leather ferns,
Kozo sushi, Zippy's chili
and Kentucky Fried Chicken.
"Don't bring any more cakes,"
your sister-in-law had told us.

You, Lynn, and I have talked to each other
for thirty-four years, since we were eleven.
Through boyfriends, and marriages,
through births, infertility, and guilt over deaths
of parents, of a child, of dreams.
"Everybody's married, everybody . . . not me," she said.
"Maybe you lucky," you told her.
"Alzheimer's and she can't even brush her teeth anymore,"
she complained.
"My father said, 'Stay through the night.' But he said it every night
and I didn't and he died," I confessed.
"We understand," we nodded.
"Don't say you understand the death of a child,
because you can't,
nobody can understand," you whispered.
We would run away together. We three
to restaurants four times a year.
to sit together again, to talk.

Ten years ago, you and Lynn
came to my hospital room.
We huddled together on my hospital bed,
surrounded by bouquets of flowers.
"I don't need to go to my funeral," I said.
"Just look at all these flowers. This is what it's going to look like."
"Cancer is not the end of life," you said.
"Be strong, don't baby yourself.
Try to get on your feet again," she said.
"But my cousins come and bring flowers and cry," I whined.
"We cannot know God's plan," you said.
Those were your words,
I remember.

Now it's Lynn and I who walk
slowly up your driveway.
Inside the house,
your husband and his golfing friends
sit at the dining room table
desperately insulting each other,
seeking comfort.
"Eh, food!" he greets us
and we hurry inside,
dispense our hugs,
and gratefully escape
into your kitchen.

Your two teenaged sons
sit on the couch, bookends
leaning in toward each other.
The only women in your house,
we take over the kitchen counters,
I, moving quickly, claim the job
of doing dishes at your sink.
Lynn, more familiar with your house,
opens your new cabinets,

sorts the disorder in your dish racks
and puts things away.
Soon, cardboard pizza boxes,
discarded foil and Saran wrap,
strewn about like emotions,
are cleaned off your counters and bundled away,
beer cans are emptied and rinsed, paper towel nests
swept into a green leaf and lawn trash bag.

We serve the food we've brought with us
"Paper plates," your husband says,
"just like always." He stands for some moments as
the weight of what cannot be continued
crushes him into silence.

Lynn and I, dishtowels in hand,
stand firm in the kitchen,
protected by tradition.
We remember the old women,
hair pulled back in buns,
bodies hidden in gray dresses printed with tiny flowers,
who came to our houses at each female's death.
Like them
we clean, serve food,
and talk gently about nothing,
"The cat looks like a manapua," we say
"Too many snacks."
"Maybe I can get in one last round of golf," your husband finally says.
"Yes," we reassure him, "it's important to get away and relax."
"I'm trying to get my mother to move in with us," he adds.
"But she doesn't want to leave her neighborhood."
"Give it time," we advise, nodding.
"We cannot know God's plan."
These are your words that we offer.
We remember them.

The scent of orchids and chrysanthemums
and irises and lilies, from ten bouquets in the house,
rises, and fills us.
We rinse your sponges and go back to work.
We clean your stove,
wipe your refrigerator's double doors,
wash the used cups and forks.
I use the scouring cloth
to rub watermarks off your faucet.
And polish it to a soft sheen.
Finally, I rinse out and stack your wedding china
on dishcloths.
Lynn polishes and arranges
dessert forks and coffee spoons precisely.
They sit ready to serve the Lutheran Church Ladies
who will arrive tomorrow.
We scour out the sink,
we wash, wring out and square fold the wiping cloths.
This is the last favor that we can do for you.

Your husband and sons
have gone silently to bed.
Lynn and I are the only ones left.
We let ourselves out quietly
into the night.
Your house is on a hillside
and the darkness surrounds us.
The Makaliʻi, little eyes, shine in the curving sky above.
The streetlights burn like the embers
nestled in white ashes
on Oʻahu's central plain below.
We sit together in Lynn's car in your driveway.
We pass the Kleenex box and wipe our tears.
Lynn is the only one I can think of to tell this to.
I lean against her arm and whisper,
"If I die first,

before you serve anybody from my kitchen,
don't forget to rinse the cockroach droppings
off the plates."
Lynn, red nose nestled in white Kleenex,
looks at me and smiles,
"And you be sure to do the same for me," she says.
"You remember to do the same for me."

Bakeru

We're sitting in the front row, dressed in black. I'm looking at the flowers. The funeral wreath we purchased this morning stands next to the coffin. It is paved with white chrysanthemums and interspersed with sprays of white orchids. There is a black banner across it. "Beloved Father" is written on the banner in white letters, and below this is the Chinese character for "Father," which is pronounced *"Otōsan"* in Japanese. I look over at my husband's father's body. Papa looks just like he's asleep but there must be blood that has settled under the skin at the back of his ears because they are the color of bruised plums. That color is so different from the chalky gray mask that is now his face.

I remember some of these Chinese characters or kanji from Japanese school. I can still picture the flowing lines of *kawa*, the word for river, and the branches and roots of the word *ki*, which means tree. The word *hana* blooms in my mind. And then I am startled by the word *bakeru*. The lower half of the kanji character for *hana*, or flower, is pronounced *bakeru*. It is composed of a sign which means man and a curved line that looks like a body wrapped for burial. *Bakeru* can mean a change of form, or it can mean a spirit re-entering the world after death. In the character for flower, the man and the body sit under a horizontal line, which represents the earth. The horizontal line is pierced by two vertical lines, which signify two new blades of grass growing. As a child I always thought the kanji for flower was a serious thing, and this feeling was reinforced in my mind by the fact that we only gave flowers to elementary school teachers and family altars.

The restrained fragrance of orchids enfolds us. The Buddhist priest in brocaded gold robes is explaining that white flowers offer their virtue on our behalf. The priest begins chanting his sutra slowly then suddenly begins a new section with a change in rhythm. At the funeral director's signal, the master of ceremonies calls for the mourners to make their offerings of incense. My mother-in-law sitting beside us stirs and sits up straight. She folds the neatly typed list in her lap and seems to gather herself in. She has been worried about this moment since the afternoon Papa died.

She was driving him to the doctor when he slumped over in the seat beside her. She drove as fast as she could and got him to the emergency room all right, but he died in the hospital while the doctors were all gathered around his bed.

She has been his nurse the past twenty-five years, since the diabetes and the blindness and the heart trouble and the asthma. She's cooked him end-less variations of saltless meals, collected a wall full of cookbooks and a stack of mimeographed sheets emblazoned with alternative medicine's latest trends. McDougall's diet, Winters tea, *noni*, aloe, *obako*, white vinegar, raisins soaked in gin, brown rice, the bran of a dozen grains, she's read about and tried each one. She even learned from the physical therapist to cup the mucus out of his lungs by pounding gently on his back.

We gathered in Mama's living room on the night of Papa's death, her two sons and one daughter and their husband and wives. In the kitchen, she washed out his last dishes at her sink, using the sponge from the plastic tofu container and the soapy water from the *sembei* tub. She opened the rice cooker and scooped out the first of the new rice she insisted on cooking for our dinner. She arranged the white grains into a mound in a brass offering bowl and set it in front of the Buddhist altar in the living room. She had tended this altar for the past forty-five years. The picture of the Buddha on the upper shelf smiled out over the pictures of Papa's parents. Mama paused there, after straightening the stems of red anthuriums in a green glass vase. I realized it was the first time I'd seen her stop moving since Papa's death.

"Papa's father was married two times," she said to no one and all of us. "His first wife died and left some children. And he had a second wife and they had more children. I don't know all about their family." She paused. "What if when we call the relatives to give Papa *senko* at the funeral, what if I get the order wrong, and I leave someone out or I don't know one of the sister's married name. Papa would be so mad." She shrank into herself. She sounded near tears for the first time. We looked toward her, but she did not cry.

The next morning, we sat silently beside her at the Hosoi Funeral Home as she repeated her concerns. "I married him and he was the oldest son," she told Clifford Hosoi, looking not into his eyes but down at the patterns of the flowered couch. "Papa never talked about his father's other family. I don't even know all their names," she confessed quietly to the beige blossoms. Clifford, in a Hawaiian funeral director's quiet reverse-print aloha shirt, listened sympathetically.

"Maybe I can find something that will help," he said as he left the room with a smile. He returned with a dusty, discolored old card.

"This is the record of your husband's father's funeral in 1935. All the names and information are here." He handed her the card and she stared at it in surprise.

She read the faint blue ink. "Yes, this is Papa's sister, and his stepmother, and all the second family's children."

"And here are the records of the other funerals in their family until just last year," he said, drawing out other cards from his desktop file.

Mama sat with the cards spread out in front of her. We all warmed ourselves in her first relieved smile.

The emcee, Mr. Ono, is ready to call out the names for the offering of incense now. He has a card in his hand that lists, in my sister-in-law's precise accountant's handwriting, the names of all the members of both sides of the Nakamura family. Mama's checked and rechecked the list ten, twenty, or thirty times. First the emcee will call all Papa's brothers and their families, with the oldest brother first, then his sisters and their families, in order by their ages. Then he'll call all Mama's brothers then her sisters. All the relatives will offer incense in family groups.

"The order is important," Mama has told us. Now the list is perfect. Mama's checked it over and over; she knows it by heart. The emcee clears his throat and calls the first name: "Mrs. Yuuko Nakamura and family," he announces. Mama sits looking puzzled. It is the first time they have ever called our family using her name and not Papa's. Mama's forehead wrinkles in concentration. She turns toward us and scans our faces. It is as if she is looking for something that she has lost. The emcee stirs nervously. Moments pass, she does not rise. A murmur passes through the row upon row of somberly dressed mourners. Suddenly, my husband who is her eldest child, stands up and looks back over the heads of the assembly. Then he leans down and takes Mama's arm. She rises, slowly, and bows in acceptance. The rest of us stand quickly and huddle behind them. Mama's sons and daughter, their wives, husband, and children.

"Mrs. Yuuko Nakamura and family," the emcee intones again. We walk to the brass cauldrons in front of Papa's casket. My husband stops and Mama goes forward alone to lift the first handful of incense. She gathers the grains of sandalwood in her fingers and gives Papa his first offering. We follow in order, oldest son, second son, and daughter, with families in tow. We scatter our incense quietly, then turn and walk back to our seats in the front row. The emcee, list in hand, is confidently chanting the names of the rest of the family. They file past the altar to make their offerings then come to shake our hands in condolence. The evening is warm, and I can smell the subtle fragrance of chrysanthemums and orchids, I think of the word *bakeru* again and I remember that it is the first character in the Japanese word *kagaku,* which means "changes in elements" and is the Japanese name for the science of chemistry. My old Japanese school-teacher, back bent and stooped over, approaches us and, as I shake his smooth dry hand, I remember *bakeru* is the second character in the word *bunka,* which is what the Japanese call "culture." The mourners file by surrounded by the scent of incense and the fragrance of flowers. The coffin, the family, the mourners, the brocade-draped priests, the offering table. They are all part of *bunka,* which blooms continually, changes constantly, and enfolds us all.

Funeral Plan

Recently, people in my family have been refusing to have funerals. They've been buried with no more than their nuclear families to witness the deed. In some cases, they have requested that their ashes be scattered offshore at their favorite fishing spots. In other cases, I'm not sure if they've been buried at all. Used to be people had a funeral when they died. The whole community would come to the funeral dressed in black suits and dresses that were perfumed by mothballs. Each family would send a representative to sign the family name and address in one of three or four funeral books lined up on a reception table. The family representative would sign in, then leave an envelope entitled "With Deepest Sympathy" with one of the friends of the family of the deceased, who were sitting at the *choba* or funeral reception table. Each of the little envelopes contained exactly the same amount of money the deceased had given to their family at the last funeral he or she had attended. Everyone consulted their funeral books as soon as they heard that someone had died. The family used the money in the little envelopes to pay for the coffin, the headstone, and the food for the funeral reception. It was one of the things we could count on; members of the community knew they had a funeral plan stored in the hearts and bank accounts of all of the other members of their extended family and all the extended families that made up the community. That's the way it was.

My Uncle John didn't have a funeral when he died. My cousin Karen, whose mother is Uncle John's wife's sister, says that his wife said he didn't want a funeral service. Uncle John's daughter, a music teacher, eventually called us to tell us the exact location of her father's grave. I keep reminding myself to go and search for it. I keep wondering why he didn't have a funeral. Maybe my Uncle John knew my mother never really understood him. Maybe because he was a G.I. Bill–educated scientist he donated his body to science and didn't want his wife to have to deal with all the relatives' questions about what might have happened. Maybe there were too many religions in his family: Episcopalian, Catholic, Congregationalist, Mormon, Shinto, and Buddhist, and he thought there might be hard feelings if he was buried in one religion and not another. Maybe after fighting so hard for American freedom in World War II, he wanted the freedom to walk away into the sunset—alone. It's been five years but I still feel funny that I couldn't go to a funeral for Uncle John.

The earliest memory I can retrieve of my third uncle is that he was smiling and soft. His hands were soft, not hard like my dad's hands. My dad was a mechanic. His hands smelled of gasoline, axle grease, and motor oil and felt hard as the iron wrenches he used every day. My uncle had soft hands and I once ran away from him when he tried to hug me because his hands felt like my mother's. "White collar, administrator," my mother said. "Makes more than Daddy and me put together every month. He has a master's degree." She didn't say much more than that, but I know it made an impression on me because the man I married also has a master's degree.

Yet, remembering him now, I think that even if his hands were soft, his heart must have been strong and tough because of the things that belonged to him that I once found hidden in my Grandpa's closet. Grandpa's room was once the room Uncle John shared with his older brother. I remember that my cousin Pam and I sneaked into Grandpa's room and explored the closet one rainy day when we were seven. Way at the back of the closet, behind Grandpa's *tabako*-smelling shirts and pants, I found an olive-green army helmet with khaki webbing inside. Pam and I took turns wearing it and hitting each other over the head with our toys just to feel the thuds they made against the metal. We were fascinated that the thuds couldn't reach our skulls because of the protective webbed strands. When we got bored with the helmet, we searched some more and found a pocket-sized Bible, a small flag with a star on it, some ribbons and medals and, finally, wonderfully wrapped in an old yellowing pillowcase, a dagger. It was silvery metal and had a black-and-white enameled swastika on the handle. I remember taking the sheath in my hand and pulling out the blade, but I don't know if it was sharp because it was just then that my Grandpa, made curious by our absence, walked into the room looking for us. After that, I remember scoldings and re-bundlings and the closet door closing and Pam and me being quickly hustled outside to spend the rest of the day playing in the hothouse.

"Four forty-second Regimental Combat Team," my mother said. "My brothers were in the Army during World War II. They picked up all that stuff when they were in Italy and France."

The next thing I remember about my uncle is something I think only I can remember. Once, when I was maybe five years old, my uncle knocked at our door late at night. I remember coming out of my bedroom into the buttery yellow light of the parlor and seeing him standing just inside the door talking to my mother. I must have been told to go back to bed because the next thing

I remember is that only the kitchen light was on in the whole house. I was in bed trying to listen to people talking, but it was hopeless and I fell asleep.

"Had a fight with his wife," my mother said later. "I told him that this was real life, not the movies, and that if he was going to divorce, he better do it quick before they have any kids. But he just said, 'You don't know her; you don't understand her heart.'" My mother squinted one eye slightly at the memory, then continued, "Love that's why, he must be in love with her." She frowned at the impractical nature of her brother's decisions. Maybe that night is the reason why we never saw much of my uncle and aunt throughout my childhood.

I think that even though he was part of my mother's family, Uncle John must have had a romantic side. I remember searching around in my mother's lingerie drawer and finding a peach-colored clamshell wrapped in tissue paper. Parts of the outside of the shell had been carved away so that the shell was transformed into a beautiful woman's face. Some of the original chalky white exterior of the shell remained and was carved into the swirling curls of the woman's upswept hairdo. More of the shell had been carved away so that the woman's face and cheeks glowed with the smooth translucence of the middle layers of the shell. The woman's cream-colored skin stood out against a soft peach background that was actually the innermost layer of the clamshell. I used to sneak into my mother's room and unwrap the cameo often. I liked to trace the swirls of the woman's hair and feel the smooth, cool curve of her cheeks. The shell cameo smelled wonderful too because my mother kept it with another tissue-wrapped bundle of thin glass vials.

The small vials were narrower than my baby finger and each was sealed with red wax. The color of the liquid in the vials ranged from very dark to almost transparent shades of rusty pink, the color of tea brewed from rose petals. Over the years, oil had seeped out of the edges of the sealing wax caps and gelled with the dust of the tissue paper and lingerie drawers. This residue smelled of musk and ancient flower petals. When I inhaled it, I dreamed of satin and taffeta ball gowns and movie kisses. The fragrance was so different from the subdued scent of my grandfather's orchids. I guess my Uncle John had bought the cameos in Italy and the perfume in France when he was a soldier and had carried them back with him for his sisters. Pam reported that her mother had similar things hidden in her bedroom drawers.

Maybe because my uncle was a romantic, he married a beautiful woman.

My aunt was stunning. She and her sisters were all admired as great beauties in the late 1940s. I remember my aunt at my grandmother's funeral in 1956. My grandparents' house was filled with people dressed in black outfits that smelled like camphor and mothballs. My grandmother's coffin, draped with soft white netting, was sitting in the upstairs parlor. There were orchids, chrysanthemums, lilies, and anthuriums everywhere. The coffin smelled like medicine and I didn't like the antiseptic odor, especially because it was covered by the overwhelming fragrance of the blossoms. It was as creepy as the white tulle that covered my grandmother's body, which was so still and didn't move. I did like the woody scent of sandalwood incense that floated comfortingly around the brass bowl on the altar in front of the coffin. Everyone who came into the house went up to the altar, knelt, picked up slender green sticks of incense and lighted them in the flame of a votive candle flickering in a ruby red cup. They then chanted, "Namu Amida Butsu," while waving the sticks of incense to extinguish the petals of flame that bloomed on their tips and inserting the fragrantly smoldering rods into the brass container. They bowed their heads into the swirling strands of smoke and said, "Namu Amida Butsu," again as they put their hands together in prayer.

When my uncle and aunt arrived at the funeral, the other mourners paused to look at them. My aunt was wearing a black taffeta dress that had obviously been purchased from a store like Carol and Mary. It had a belted waist and she was wearing a cameo pin on her lapel. She looked like a movie star from Paris and smelled like roses. My mother and her sister, wearing home-sewn black polyester crepe dresses, could only stare in wonder.

My uncle and aunt were a 1950s Nisei couple. They both used only their English names. They both had college degrees; they both had jobs that paid a thousand dollars a month. They bought a house in a community in which the rest of the owners had to approve new purchasers. They installed a swimming pool in their backyard. We visited them maybe twice that I can remember. My father and I escaped from the house and walked a block down the street to a pier by the water. I remember the sea cucumbers that lived in the mud under the luxury boat pier. My dad and I spent the afternoon poking the sea cucumbers with sticks. When we prodded the sea cucumbers, they would turn themselves inside out in an effort to preserve their lives.

My father was a mechanic and there was always a car or two inside our fenced yard with its engine gutted and unraveling around his workbench. He also kept a hunting dog and once kept a goat too "to help with the California grass," he said. But I think he kept it as a souvenir of his last hunting trip to remind him never to go hunting again. Our house and our family would never have fit into an exclusive community.

My father's family always had large, noisy parties. These were usually held in someone's garage. My father's brothers and his sisters had not gone to college. Only my oldest uncle finished high school while my father and the rest of his brothers became apprentices and learned trades. His one surviving sister married early and had a large family. It was not until my cousins' generation that, led by my cousin David and his sisters in 'Ewa and the Ota girls in Kalihi, we began to get our college degrees. A party on my dad's side featured bottles of soda and beer on ice in the cement laundry tubs, a buffet table in the house from which everyone loaded their food on paper plates, all the women chatting in the kitchen and all the men sitting outside in the garage, and children and dogs running wild in the yard drinking soda straight from the bottles and playing under the moon.

Nowadays, I am known as one of the women who goes to funerals. Going to a funeral begins with a phone call from one or another of my cousins. It then proceeds to a mad rush to the closet to check for a black, brown, or blue outfit that looks somber enough and yet still fits. Everyone in a family must wear a suitable outfit.

"Wear your shirt on the outside over your pants so people cannot see that you cannot button them!"

"No, you cannot wear that shirt because it shows your belly button. Yes, I know it's the only black one you have."

"No, you cannot wear slippers and you cannot wear Skechers even though they are black!"

"Damn, this used to fit perfectly, what—three years ago?"

After finding acceptable outfits, we dash to Longs for a sympathy card and to a bank machine for a respectable but not ostentatious amount of cash.

"No make big shot and give too much or their family going have hard time returning the money if somebody in your family pass away."

My cousins and I are the ones who show up at mortuaries and burials. These women, in their forties, fifties, and sixties, are good girls who do the expected things. They either got married or remained single to care for their frail, elderly mothers. They not only go to funerals, they also go to the family gravesites every holiday to offer flowers, and to wash and tend the graves. I am the bad girl who doesn't go. The good girls check up on me very subtly. They suspect that I shirk my familial duty.

"We went to the graveyard on Memorial Day and put torch ginger on our dad's grave and your parents' grave too," they say. I smile gratefully and thank them, but they are not mollified. "There were white anthuriums there when we got there," they continue. "Those were probably yours, yea?" they prod.

"Yea, we took all the kids to clean the gravesite on Memorial Day," one woman says, nodding.

"Had stephanotis and red torch ginger there when we got there," another says.

"We brought the white anthuriums," a third chimes in. "We cleaned out some old protea that were already there." They look at me expectantly. They raise their eyebrows when I say nothing. It is always the same. Uncle John's wife and daughter show up to all the funerals too. Every time I see them, I think that not having a funeral was not their idea, and I wonder about Uncle John.

My cousin's husband Ed really knew how to have a funeral. His son Mike gave a wonderful eulogy listing all the things that his father had counted as blessings. Besides his wife, his children, his grandchildren, his family and their extended families, Mike said that his father Ed, a thirty-three year University of Hawai'i football season ticket holder, was grateful that even though he had cancer, he had made it into the June Jones football era! As we stood at Ed's graveside, after the 21-gun military salute and flag ceremony, I couldn't help contrasting the way we celebrated Ed's life with Uncle John's lack of a funeral. The final memory I have of Ed is the one of his wife, my cousin June, kissing the face of his gold and bronze urn, of his children and grandchildren surrounding her as a worker lowered the urn into the earth. The final memory I have of my Uncle John, on the other hand, is only that one moment in the movie theater, after the credits have crossed the screen, after the music has stopped playing, the moment when the screen, which was once so bright, has finally gone dark.

Sakura

The Japanese immigration officer looked grim as he studied my tourist and military passports. He then asked me random questions in English. "Where were you born? Why have you come to Japan? How long will you stay?" He looked sternly at the bundle in my hands, which I had wrapped with a black scarf. "What is that you are carrying?" he asked.

"*Ihai*," I said. "My parents' *ihai*." The immigration officer frowned.

"Unwrap them," he ordered. I unwrapped two carved wooden Buddhist tablets that bore the spirit names of my deceased mother and father. He looked at me with distaste as though I had committed some breach of etiquette.

"*O-IHAI*," he said to me slowly, using the honorific address for the objects I carried. He frowned his disapproval as he stamped my passport.

I had arrived at Narita Airport on a chartered TWA flight from Hawai'i to Japan. As I walked into the busy international terminal, I thought of my grandfather, who had often gazed at me when I was a little girl and had said, "Mei-chan, you have my mother's face." I felt that I, an ignorant foreigner, was bringing my great-grandmother's face and my parents' spirits back to Japan.

Six months earlier, I had married Mike, a *sansei* guy from Palama who was a major in the United States Air Force. Like me, he had been divorced. Like me, he was looking to start over. What better way than with an assignment in an interesting foreign place. "So, why are you marrying him?" asked my friend Gloria as we walked our dogs around the neighborhood. "I thought you were looking for a soul mate, for romance, for sparks."

"Because maybe nobody else is going to ask me, I've had cancer, I'm going to be forty, and he's getting stationed in Japan," I found myself saying. She narrowed her eyes and stared at me. Gloria is my friend who found a puppy on the North Shore and paid $700 for surgery to fix his broken leg. She is a woman who finally spent $250,000 to buy a house to keep her dog in after she found that no one would rent to a woman who owned an 80-pound Labrador–pit bull.

"Well, it might work out," she said finally. Gloria is the most loyal person I know. I thought of Gloria and her dog Rickie a lot during the nine-hour flight from Hawai'i to Tokyo. I also thought of my German shepherd, Addie, who was stuck in the airplane's cargo hold. Addie had been my companion after my divorce. She had been my chemotherapy dog. She and I had inhabited the house my mother left me.

Mike had called me long distance every day since he had left for Tokyo. He said that he would leave the airbase he was stationed at one hour before my scheduled arrival time and meet me at Narita Airport. After I cleared customs, I headed to the baggage claim area for my flight. I immediately saw the giant dog crate that contained my German Shepherd. Addie pawed at the steel door of her dog crate when she saw me. I couldn't let her out into the terminal so I caressed her through the cage door. I found a luggage cart and loaded the dog crate and my two suitcases onto its wheeled platform. I wrapped the wooden memorial tablets in my sweater and then again in my overcoat and stowed the bundle in my carry-on bag. I trundled the whole load back into the main terminal. I was looking for the Armed Forces Morale, Welfare and Recreation (MWR) desk that Mike told me would be next to one of the exit doors.

"Has Major Nagata left a message for me?" I asked the American clerk at the MWR desk.

"No, ma'am, no messages. If you're going to the Air Force base, you need to get on the MWR bus in one hour. It's the last bus out of here tonight," the young man warned me.

"My husband said he would meet me," I tried to explain. "How long does it take to drive to Yokota from here?"

"Hard to say, ma'am, with Tokyo traffic and all. Could be one hour, could be three hours. If there's been an accident on one of them freeways, could be tomorrow morning. You can never be really sure." He frowned. It was 1989, and we were without the instant cellphone communication that everyone relies on today. "Look, I'd say wait for him until the bus leaves, but I would feel safer if you got on the bus and got to the base tonight," he concluded.

So it was that one hour later, Addie, my dog, and I were loaded onto a large blue military bus for a three-hour trip through the Tokyo highway system. I sat with my carry-on bag containing my parents' *o-ihai* on my lap and worried about my dog. She had endured the nine-hour plane flight and now she was stowed with other luggage in the back of the military bus. I had shared a small amount of water with her at the airport, but I hadn't known where to buy food at the terminal. I wondered where Mike was and how he would find out where we had gone. So far, my adventure in Japan was more nightmare than I had bargained for.

Three hours later, we were off-loaded at the Military Airlift Command (MAC) terminal on the Tokyo Air Force Base. I checked on Addie, who looked forlorn but calm in her airline crate. I spotted a small fast-food café in the terminal and went over to buy hamburgers and water. Addie and I ate our first meal on Japanese soil together. She was overjoyed to be receiving something other than dog food; I was trying to hold down my hysteria at not being able to find Mike. After our meal, I slipped a collar and leash on Addie and walked her outside the terminal building. I stared out across the yellow and blue runway lights, shivered in the January night air, and realized that I was stranded alone in a country in which I knew only one person, and I did not know where that one person was.

"Are you Mike Nagata's wife?" A tall, thin, middle-aged American man in a polo shirt, jeans, and tennis shoes asked me as I headed back toward Addie's dog crate.

"Yes, how do you know?" I answered.

"Well, Major Nagata called me from Narita Airport about fifteen minutes ago and asked me to find his wife and German shepherd at the MAC terminal. The German shepherd is easy to spot." The man smiled. "Welcome to Tokyo. My name is Bob Perry; I'm a major in Mike's office. Seems like there was an accident on the freeway and Mike only just arrived at Narita a short time ago. The MWR folks told him that you and your dog had left on the bus."

Soon, Addie was enjoying the Perrys' fenced backyard and I was sitting in warm and cozy cement-block family housing watching the Armed Forces' English language news program with Bob and Janice Perry. Just when Jay Leno began his monologue, Mike knocked on the Perrys' front door. Addie yelped a joyful greeting, and I rushed to hug him in what must have been more of a stranglehold than an embrace.

"Thanks, Bob." Mike managed to pry me loose and shake Bob's hand.

"Where were you? Addie and I thought you were dead," I said tearfully.

"There was an accident on the highway, and a roadblock," Mike explained. "I had to go around it, but I ended up taking the wrong overpass and ended up in Hachioji before I realized what happened."

"You should have checked the map before you started," I wept. I looked up at Mike's face. I could see he was staring apologetically at our hosts. "I'm sorry, Janice, I'm being ridiculous," I said in embarrassment. "I don't know why I'm acting like this after you and Bob saved us and Mike has finally found us." To my surprise, Janice smiled warmly at me.

"It's okay, honey," she said soothingly. "You're just having your first assignment. Everybody goes through a first assignment." She wrote a phone number on a piece of paper and pressed it into my hand. "You just call me anytime you need to talk," she said.

Several hours later, we were in Mike's one-room accommodations in the Bachelor Officers' Quarters (BOQ). Addie was in mandatory one-week quarantine at the base vet's compound.

"Don't worry, it will all look better in the morning," Mike said. "I gotta get some sleep 'cause I gotta go to the office in the morning." Mike had stowed my suitcases under the bed, and I hung up my coat and stuffed my carry-on bag with my parents' *o-ihai* in it onto the top shelf of the closet. I went to the bathroom to shower and change and spent a good long time under the running water trying to wash away my tears. When I returned to the room, Mike was fast asleep.

The next morning, after Mike went to work, I walked around the BOQ complex. I found the small diner Mike had told me about and ordered *cha-han*, fried rice with eggs for breakfast. Next, I walked around outside, feeling the January chill in the air. Dressed in sweater, coat, jeans, and shoes, I still felt the cold but decided to keep walking. The trees around the base were bare and brown. Only the pine trees were still green. The grass was a sickly yellow. I pulled the hood of my sweater over my head and put my hands into my pockets. Inside the base, I could have been walking anywhere in America. The buildings were red brick and the signs were all in English. I walked past the base library, post office, Laundromat, and McDonalds. About one hundred yards away, beyond a perimeter fence, though, I could see houses and shops crowded together. I could see but could not read a riot of signs written in kanji. Beyond the fence, I could see Japan. I felt a small surge of excitement.

Mike came home early for lunch and announced that he had taken the next two days off. That afternoon, we attended a class about the treaty that sets down rules of behavior for American dependents stationed in Japan. Next, Mike went to register Addie and me as his dependents, and I attended a class on basic etiquette and the Japanese currency system. Last, while Mike was making arrangements for off-base housing, I attended a class about driving in Japan.

When Mike came to pick me up, I tried driving the Japanese Toyota Tercel he had bought. The steering wheel was on the right side of the front seat instead of the left side like my Toyota Corolla in Hawai'i. I also had to drive on the left side of the road, instead of the right side. I am left-handed and I was very anxious about trying to drive in what to me seemed like the world on the other side of a mirror. Once I started doing it, though, sitting on the wrong side of the car and driving on the wrong side of the road were not so bad. After a few blocks, it began to seem normal. I drove to the veterinarian's compound and we visited Addie in her cage inside a heated building. A very nice volunteer named Pam showed us around and assured us that Addie would be fed two meals a day and exercised in the morning and evening. Addie looked unhappy but let us leave without whimpering. Mike had been right, Japan began to look better on this second day. That night in the BOQ, my brain, confused by the time change, put my body to sleep at 8:00 in the evening. Mike had to watch the news alone.

"*Okaikei wa achira no ho ni itashimasu,*" the saleswoman said to me the next day in Tokyo. I was trying to buy an egg salad sandwich in a small coffee shop. Mike and I had taken an "Explore Tokyo by Train" tour led by an MWR guide named Mr. Murakami. It was the first time that I had made contact with a native Japanese person who did not speak English. The woman looked at me expectantly, waiting for me to follow her directions. She was talking to my great-grandmother's face with every expectation that she would be understood. I had actually understood only about one third of what she said. Mr. Murakami came and stood beside me.

"She says that the cash register is on the other side of the store, and you must go and pay over there," he explained.

"Oh, okay," I said to him and smiled in embarrassment at the woman. She squinted at me with a puzzled expression on her face. I bowed to her and retreated with my sandwich to the line in front of the cash register.

"Tokyo is so large that the fastest way to get around is by train," Mr. Murakami told our group of American newcomers in the coffee shop. "On the train, you can get to Narita Airport from the base in about 40 minutes," he said.

"It took me three hours to get out there and one hour to get back on the highway!" Mike exclaimed.

"Why did you not take the train?" asked Mr. Murakami.

"I was trying to pick up my wife and dog from the airport," Mike explained.

"No, no," said Mr. Murakami putting up his two index fingers in the sign of the cross. "No dogs can go on board the train!"

Tokyo made me anxious. Not only was it the largest, most crowded city I had ever seen, many highways and train tracks rose high above the streets, while subway trains ran on multiple levels beneath the roadbeds as well. I felt that people who did not speak English were pressing in against me from all directions. I was relieved when we boarded the train back to the base.

It was late by the time we got back to the BOQ. After the crush of activity during the last two days, I was determined to make some time that evening to get reacquainted with Mike. Just as we settled down together on the couch at 9:00, however, the phone rang. It was Pam from the veterinarian's compound.

"Addie won't go back into her cage," she said. "I've tried dragging her, I've tried bribing her with food, but she won't go in. She's just sitting outside by the front gate, looking down the street." I looked guiltily at Mike, wondering what he would say.

"Come on," he said, grabbing his coat, "she misses us." We found Addie huddled against the front gate of the vet's compound. She whined and jumped against the bars as soon as we got out of the car. "Sorry, Ad, I bet you thought we forgot about you," said Mike as he stroked the dog's fur. We went back into the building with her following close at our heels. We stayed while she ate a heavy snack back in her cage. I was impressed that Mike was so willing to leave his warm room to go comfort a dog. After we drove back to the BOQ, I held his hand as we walked back up to our room. Later that evening, as we revived our roles as husband and wife, I was glad that my parents' o-ihai were still safely stored in the closet. For the first time, I felt Gloria had been right. This might work out after all.

It was so cold when I opened my eyes that I could see the mist generated by my breath hanging in the air above me. I was warm enough though. I was lying on a bed that we had rented from MWR covered by two blankets, an electric blanket, and a three-inch thick Japanese futon. I was dressed in socks, tights, jeans, two T-shirts, and a hooded jacket. Mike, who was lying beside me, was similarly dressed. I fumbled for the electric blanket control and turned up the heat. When the bed felt nice and toasty, I emerged from the blankets and put my feet into my house slippers so that my feet would not make contact with the icy wooden floor. Addie looked at me from her nest beside our bed. She was curled up on a sleeping bag that had been folded over twice and covered with a fluffy sheepskin rug. She was wearing a dog sweater over her back and chest that Mike's mother had knitted and sent to us from Hawai'i. Addie and I sprinted down the hall to the bathroom. I pulled down my jeans and jumped a couple of feet into the air when my bare skin touched the toilet seat in the unheated bathroom. This was my first morning in our house in American Village.

Mike had tried to get us into family housing on the base and even now, we were moving up the waiting list. The problem was that we had a dog and needed a townhouse with a fenced yard. These were hard to come by in winter, Mike explained, because the families that usually occupied townhouses moved during the summer, so that their children would not miss attending school. American Village was a housing complex about two miles away from the base. A Japanese businessman owned the complex and he had been renting houses to Americans since the end of World War II.

"We're living on the economy," said Mike. The house was clean and modern. But it was very large by Japanese standards. This was the problem. The house was heated by propane, which was very expensive. There was only one propane heater in the place, in the living room/dining room area in the front of the house. The bedrooms were located in the rear of the house and heating them with the propane heater was very costly. Mike learned from the people in his office that the most economical way to heat the back rooms was to use kerosene space heaters. In addition, electric blankets could be used to take the chill off the bedding. However, the kerosene heater generated carbon monoxide and a window had to be left open when one was in use. Electric blankets caused problems of their own. They created an electromagnetic field, which was probably not healthy for humans sleeping under them for many hours. The solution was to heat the room with the kerosene heater for a couple of hours before bedtime, then heat the bed with the electric blanket about thirty minutes before getting into it. Finally, we turned off the electric blanket, turned down the kerosene heater to the lowest possible level and slept huddled together, using the traditional Japanese bedding, the thick, cotton-padded futon. We found that if we did this we would stay comfortable until morning.

"Now I know why Japanese had to invent heated toilet seats!" I screamed to Mike from the bathroom. I turned on the propane-heated hot water and washed my face and brushed my teeth. Soon, the whole bathroom was filled with beautiful warm steam. "Close the door fast when you come in here," I yelled to Mike. I then headed to the kitchen to turn up the main propane heater to warm the house and plugged in the Tiger Pot to heat water for our morning coffee. I slipped a leash on Addie and walked her around our unit so that she could take care of her morning business too. It was so cold that she walked only a few steps before emptying her bladder on a small strip of grass in the backyard. She then pulled me back up the steps and into the house.

For some reason, electricity and kerosene were inexpensive. Propane, on the other hand, was very high-priced. Bob and Janice had warned us that our fuel bill could easily exceed two hundred dollars if we were not careful. Microwave ovens were wonderful, as were electric rice cookers and hot water pots. Since the stove used propane, I found that dried ramen made with water heated in an electronic pot made an inexpensive breakfast and *ochazuke*, tea-soaked rice, made a good lunch.

I put my parents' *o-ihai* in the sunny, front bay window of the house. If I had not become a Christian, I would have set up a small statue of the Buddha and offered the altar incense and the first serving from every pot of rice that I cooked. I have always felt awkward about placing the *o-ihai* in an incomplete altar. We drove to the base to do our laundry and visit the commissary that first week. When we returned, I offered my parents' spirits a bouquet of *manryo*, Japanese holly, with glossy green leaves and bright red berries, which I purchased from the base grocery store. Even Christians offered flowers to their parents' memories, I reasoned. After four weeks in Japan, I was content; it was then that Mike told me he was going to Korea for two weeks of temporary duty.

The morning that Mike left, I kept myself busy unpacking our small shipment of household goods. A larger shipment remained in storage and we would not see it again until we moved into our permanent base housing. The house was built so that it was warmed by the morning and afternoon sun. I was able to turn off the propane heater by about 9:30. I went on working on the house until it was dusk and the cold began to creep up through the floors again.

Evening has always been a very lonely time for me. I was afraid to drive the car without Mike, so I was pretty much tied to the area around American Village. I knew no one in the housing complex and had no job, so I would remain pretty much isolated until Mike got back. I was thirty-nine. I would be forty that summer. I had given up a life in Hawai'i where I had a job and could travel freely. I missed being able to get on the telephone to call my friend Gloria and meet her to take our dogs for a long walk. I sat on my borrowed

MWR couch and gazed at my parents' *o-ihai*. Although it had been seven years since my father's death and three years since my mother's, I still missed them terribly. I missed Mike and I realized that his job would continue to take him away from me for weeks at a time. Why had I gotten myself in this situation? I threw a pillow at the door of the house and began to cry. Addie got up from the sheepskin rug in the living room that she had claimed as her second nest and came to lick my face.

I made a soup and rice dinner for myself and fed Addie her dog food. After dinner, I realized that Mike had usually taken Addie out for her evening walk. I put on her leash and chain and wrapped myself in a coat and we headed out into the cold. The trees in American Village had all lost their leaves and their bare branches were dark against the evening sky. Addie walked down our lane, past the trash bins. Trash was governed by rules here. Mr. Higashi, the resident manager, had explained the rules to us when we had moved in. Trash had to be separated into 'burnable' and 'unburnable' items. 'Unburnable' trash included metal and glass containers and batteries. 'Burnables' and 'unburnables' had to be bagged separately and put into the proper community receptacles. Mr. Higashi reminded me of the immigration inspector I had met at Narita Airport. He seemed to resent having to speak to us in English when our faces said that we were Japanese. I wondered what would happen if I rebelled and threw out my trash American style. Addie continued to walk down the lane toward the perimeter fence. My ears got colder and colder and began to ache as Addie kept pulling me onward. She sniffed at each clump of grass along the perimeter fence.

"This is your version of Armed Forces Television News, isn't it?" I said to her. "Hurry up and do your thing! I'm freezing!" At last, when I felt my nose beginning to go numb, Addie dropped her load. I picked it up in one of the five plastic bags I had stuffed into my pockets. We jogged back to the house past the trash bins where, in a fit of irritation, I deposited Addie's production into the unburnable container. That night, by the light of the television set, huddled up against the propane heater, I remembered the writing group I had left behind in Hawai'i. I had written some stories about my childhood, which had been published. The members of the group were always after me to write about more recent things and above all, to show my feelings. I began to write my thoughts in a journal.

I wrote about the cold, about the bare, brown tree branches, about how I missed Mike, how I missed Gloria, and how I missed my father and mother. I wrote about isolation, and doubt, about being forty and resentful that I was starting all over again. At the end of an hour, I wrote: *I am a tree without leaves, so many empty hands reaching.* I didn't know where that image had come from. The words expressed exactly how I felt, and yet I had not consciously composed them. I was intrigued.

The next morning, I woke up alone in bed, but for some reason, I was not lonely. I sprinted through my freezing morning routine and heated water for tea. I drank bright green Japanese tea from my grandfather's blue and white porcelain teacup and noticed that it tasted sweet. I had not noticed that the water in the house was as pure and sweet tasting as the artesian water that flowed from our taps in Hawai'i.

That morning, when I took Addie for a walk, a tall blonde neighbor looked my way and bowed. My grandmother's face had fooled someone again. "Hi," I said. "This is my dog Addie. We live in #307." The woman looked slightly perplexed, then she smiled broadly.

"Hi, my name is Christine, Christine Cross."

"I'm Mei Nagata," I said. "How do you stand it outside, it's so cold?"

"When you go to school in Michigan, you learn fast," she said, laughing. "Okay, first you need to dress in layers. Put cotton close to your skin, then wool over that. You also need to wear a hat or hood because you lose most of your heat from your head," Christine smiled. "I live in #309, why don't you drop in for lunch sometime?"

When Addie and I got back into our house, I went back into the bedroom and re-dressed following Christine's advice. I dressed in black tights and put on a pair of Mike's wool socks, then my thickest pair of denim jeans. On top, I put on a cotton undershirt, a cotton turtleneck sweater and over that, a wool V-neck vest and my coat. I used one of Mike's ski caps to cover my head. That evening, I didn't care if Addie took her time finding exactly the right place to do her thing; I felt I could stay outside for hours. I felt warm and invulnerable. I ran into Christine again on my evening walk and thanked her for her advice.

"Can I come along with you all?" she asked. "My husband is on temporary duty in the Philippines and I'm going stir crazy in this house." I was impressed at how easily Christine could converse with someone she just met this morning. She was about five years younger than me, in her mid-thirties. Yet, we were both stuck here in an unfamiliar country and, as American military wives, had many things in common. "So, my name used to be Christine Hardy," she said. "That was an okay name, and I had to think long and hard before I married Andy," she said as we walked along.

"Why? I've seen him only once or twice, but he seems like a nice guy," I said.

"Okay, think about it . . . I used to be Chris Hardy now I'm Chris . . . ." She paused.

"Oh, I get it," I said. "Good thing you don't have red hair," I smiled.

"And I live in fear of having twins, you know, double," she concluded. As we passed the trash containers, I told her what I had thrown into the unburnable bins. We giggled our way around the perimeter fence.

That night, after a dinner of miso soup with eggs and rice, I opened my journal again and wrote again for an hour. I sketched an outline of memories and planned to end my day with a long hot shower before jumping into my electrically toasted futon. I wrote: *the dog sleeping at my feet is now my only ocean, the blood in her veins moving in tiny tides, her even breathing soothing my heart like the rhythm of waves against the sand.* Again, I did not know where the image came from. It was as if I was observing someone else's writing. I wondered if this was the first stage of mental illness, and yet, I didn't feel ill. For the first time in many weeks, I began to feel happy.

The next morning, Christine knocked at my door. I opened it and she was waving a white piece of paper, and seemed very upset.

"20,000 yen! How much is 20,000 yen in dollars?" she asked.

"Okay, 10,000 yen is about $100," I calculated. "So, 20,000 is about $200. Why? What cost you $200?" I asked.

"I think this is the fuel bill. I found it in my mailbox this morning." I looked at the piece of paper she had been waving. My Palama Japanese School knowledge of kanji was, at best, terrible. I wished I had played less schoolyard volleyball and had studied harder.

"I think this character says '*denki*'—electricity. The charge is 3,000 yen. This other line says '*puropain*'—propane. Wow! That's 17,000 yen." Her hysteria had been transferred to me. I rushed outside to my mailbox. "Mine says only 10,000 yen, but we've only been here three weeks," I yelled as I stepped back into the house.

"Okay, that means in another week, your bill will only be about 13,000 yen," Christine said. "How are you keeping your fuel cost that low?" I thought about what we had been doing.

"We use kerosene in the back bedroom, and an electric blanket in the early evening," I said. Christine nodded vigorously.

"So do we," she said. "So I don't think it's from heating the house." I scratched my head.

"I heat water in the electric pot and have ramen noodles for breakfast," I admitted sheepishly. "I have tea over rice and heat leftovers in the microwave for lunch."

"What do you all eat for dinner?" Christine asked.

"Usually Chinese or Japanese food," I answered. "I cut everything up into thin slices. I cook the vegetables first, take them out of the pot and cook the meat. When I put the vegetables back in, everything cooks together, takes about ten minutes, tops."

"Okay, you all don't have pot roast and stew and baked chicken at night then," she said. I was horrified.

"Don't you have to bake a chicken for at least an hour?" I asked. "The stove is burning propane for all those minutes!"

"But I don't think I can feed Andy Asian food every night," Christine wailed. "You guys might be used to it, but . . . ." She looked very unhappy. "I can't make Andy eat vegetables! He's a meat-and-potatoes kind of guy. American food takes a lot of expensive propane to cook. I never thought about food that way before," she said.

"I never thought about fuel either. I always thought Asian women cut everything in small pieces so that people could eat it with chopsticks." I was suddenly impressed with my great-grandmother and her sisters. "Two thousand years of history versus two hundred years of history produces fuel-efficient cuisine," I gloated.

"Can you teach me to cook Asian-style?" Christine asked.

"Sure, but we have to get to the base so we can buy ingredients at the commissary," I said. The next day, I drove and Christine navigated; we made it all the way to the base. We started out shopping in the base exchange and planned to go to the commissary last so it would be the last stop on the way home. I bought lamb's wool-lined leather gloves, a hat, and a scarf. Christine looked unhappy as she walked up and down the aisles of the base exchange. Suddenly, in the small appliance section, I could see her mood change. She smiled slyly at me with her hands behind her back.

"I figured out how I can still have pot roast and stew without paying propane prices," Christine said triumphantly.

"You can't fight history," I said shaking my head.

"You can if you get a crock pot," she said producing a small pot she had been holding behind her. She was right. I had been cooking rice and heating water with electricity for three weeks and I still had a reasonable bill.

"I think you've just saved Andy from vegetables." I nodded at her. "Women can solve any problem." We filled our car with supplies from the exchange and the commissary and drove home. We no longer felt housebound. We felt that all things were possible as we drove home along tree-lined streets.

"Look at the branches, there are pink bumps along the twigs," I exclaimed.

"Yep, spring is coming all right. I think those are plum blossoms," said Christine, craning her neck to get a better look. "Haven't you ever seen flowers blooming in spring before?"

"There's usually always something blooming in Hawai'i," I said. "It's not like here where everything dies in the winter."

"You're gonna love what's coming up in the next few weeks," she said. "Flowers will break out all over the place. Except for the pollen, it's wonderful." I suddenly felt an excitement building inside me. If I could hang on for three more weeks, I would make it through winter.

The next day, Christine and I explored the surrounding area by car. We found a Japanese supermarket and went in. I found the food fascinating. The store was like Marukai in Hawai'i, but it contained so much more. The produce section sold ginger root and ginger shoots. There were leeks, chives, and green onions. There were fresh turnips and radishes and sprouted radish seeds. There were a hundred kinds of noodles, fresh and dried, and twenty kinds of *natto*. Although there was not much beef, there was so much fish and shellfish that I was amazed.

"Ask the saleslady what this vegetable is," Christine said, thrusting a small plastic-wrapped packet in my hand.

"I think you'll have more luck if you ask her," I said, but I knew it was useless when she pouted at me. "Really, if you ask, she will try her best to speak English. If I ask, she'll just look irritated at me and think I'm mentally defective," I whined. Christine narrowed her eyes and hardened her mouth into an irritated line.

"You have to try," she ordered. I thought hard about the best way to phrase the question. I was determined not to repeat my airport mistake again. I carefully added an honorific "o" to as many words as I could. Finally, I went up to the kindest looking clerk I could find.

"*Sumimasen*," I apologized. "*Kono o-yasai no o-namae wa nan to o-shaimasu ka?*" The woman looked at me for what seemed an eternity. I wondered in horror if I was breaking a rule by using words that usually referred to human beings when I tried to describe vegetables.

"*Kore wa warabi desu*," she said slowly and in a rather loud voice. She looked into my eyes with some concern, as if she were wondering if I had had a stroke. I bowed to her and hurried back to Christine.

"It's *warabi*, a fern shoot," I said. I had done it. I had enough language to survive. I bought my parents a small bouquet of plum blossoms surrounded by lacy ferns. The next two weeks flew by.

I drove myself to the base terminal and picked up Mike, who had arrived back in Japan from his temporary-duty assignment. He was impressed at the progress I had made. That evening, we economically shared a warm bath in our Japanese-style furo tub. I once again marveled that Mike did not seem to see my cancer scars. The deep tub let us soak in warm water up to our necks. As our giggles blossomed in the warm steam, I decided there were aspects of Japan that could be quite wonderful.

On our morning walk, Addie and I saw patches of the green tips of what might become tulips or daffodils in a neighbor's yard. When we passed the plum tree, instead of bumpy brown branches, we saw hundreds of pink blossoms, each one opened in a fragrant smile. Suddenly, there was color everywhere as green blades of grass and pink-and-white flowers seemed to have appeared overnight. What had been dead and brown one week ago was now suddenly alive again.

Christine and her husband, who had lived at American Village longer than we had, moved on base that week. "Call me!" I admonished her as I waved good-bye. She never called and I wondered why. Surprisingly, I did not miss her very much. When Mike was at work, I drove the car on short trips around the area. I studied the other Japanese housewives at the small shops. I found that if I remained quiet, most of the shopkeepers assumed that I was just another housewife. If anyone asked me a question, I tried my best to answer in monosyllables. Most days, I had only to say an occasional "*sumimasen*" and bow slightly to remain invisible. I could move about freely and observe Japan undetected, hiding behind my great-grandmother's face. I explored during the day and, when Mike was on TDY, wrote in my journal at night.

Shibui: The piercing yellows of wild running, the red streaks of laughter, the oranges of whispered secrets, the colors of childhood, fade into the brown of bloodstains drying, the grays of waiting for rice to cook, for laundry to dry, for children to fall asleep, the black of fading into a husband's shadow.

It was the end of February. The shops began to display colorful *hinamatsuri* dolls on many-tiered shelves. Plum blossoms bloomed in tiny vases on the bottom shelves, and pink and green *mochi* cut into diamond shapes stood on tiny offering plates. Musician dolls played on the next shelves, while courtier dolls dressed in colorful silk kimonos listened. On the top shelf were the emperor and empress dolls dressed in brocades and silks. Tiny golden crowns sat on their heads as they surveyed the beautiful spring scene. The plum trees outside the shop windows were dressed in glorious pink petals. March third has always been Girls' Day in Japan. This year, for the first time, I understood the happiness with which Japanese families greeted girl children, who bloomed like plum blossoms, promising to pass life on to another generation.

In early March, Mike got the good news that a townhouse on base had suddenly become available. We were able to move on base unexpectedly early. The Air Force sent Japanese movers who packed up our household goods and within two days we were in base housing. The first night was wonderful. I had all electric appliances including a washer and dryer inside my kitchen. There were three bedrooms upstairs and a large living room and kitchen downstairs. The house had central heating. The base burned fuel oil to supply hot water for the showers and steam for the radiators. After the winter in American Village, I felt that I had been promoted to heaven. We took long, long hot showers and ran around the upstairs bedrooms barefooted. I felt slightly guilty about using American quantities of fuel again. Addie could roam freely around the fenced backyard. We were all grateful to be Americans. As I cooked breakfast the next morning in my bare feet, I understood why Christine could not call me. It would have been like eating sweets in front of a diabetic—obscene.

I unwrapped my parents' *o-ihai* and set up their makeshift altar in the small upstairs bedroom. From their perch on a table, they could look out over the green courtyard between buildings and at the base road, which was lined with brown, bare-branched trees. I unwrapped a bud vase and offered my parents a sprig of deep pink plum blossoms. My father and mother had traveled all over the western United States. My uncle was a tour guide and my parents had traveled with him as far as the Grand Canyon. Their photo albums were crammed full of pictures of themselves with other retirees from all parts of the country. They had enjoyed their retirement, but my father had always refused to visit Japan. As I paused thoughtfully at the window, the doorbell rang. Addie barked urgently at the door. Mike opened it and was greeted with, "Howsit! You guys moving in? How about some Big Island Candies' shortbread?" I ran down the stairs. The man and woman standing in our doorway were vaguely familiar.

"Palama Japanese School? Volleyball?" I said hesitantly to the woman.

"Sprained fingers and copying kanji tests!" she answered laughingly. "Mei! Do you remember me, Annie Nakatani?"

"Oh, my goodness! Annie! I remember you," I said.

"Eh, Mike . . . your brother still playing basketball at Kapunahala Park?" asked her husband.

"Luke Ito! Whatchu doing down here?" said Mike. We invited the Itos into our box-filled living room. As we shared green tea, we compared life stories. Luke worked for the civilian administration of the air base. He and Annie had been stationed in Japan for the past five years. Annie helped me unpack my boxes, and soon we shared each other's kitchens as comfortably as if they were our own. While Mike and Luke went off to their jobs, Annie and I got on the train and went antique hunting all over Tokyo. Annie's mother had been born and raised in Japan. Annie grew up hearing and speaking Japanese and was much more fluent than I was. Being with her was like having a professional tour guide. We were soon as close as sisters.

The Itos had married late in life. Though she seldom spoke about it, Annie had been divorced, and this was her second marriage. Annie and I talked about everything in our world except our first marriages. We seemed to respect each other's reluctance and stayed away from asking much about the subject. Both Luke's and Annie's families had emigrated to Hawai'i from Kumamoto, Japan. One day in late March, Luke called Mike about a trip.

"Luke said we can catch a hospital flight out of the base terminal and get off at Iwakuni near Hiroshima," Mike said that afternoon. "We can rent a van from Iwakuni MWR and drive from Hiroshima to Kumamoto City."

"Are you sure you guys can figure out the roads?" I asked skeptically. "And where are we going to stay at night? I don't think they have trailer parks in Japan."

"MWR can call ahead and make reservations for us in Japanese," said Mike. "Annie and Luke want to visit an orphanage in Kumamoto City, and they wanted to know if we wanted to go along for the ride. You could go see your grandfather's hometown. I think it's close to there." I was intrigued. I had made my peace with not having children after having had cancer, so going to an orphanage did not seem particularly compelling. But I had always wanted to see the town that my grandfather was from. Now that everyone in my family who had any connection to Japan had passed away, I wondered if I would feel any connection to the place where my great-grandmother had been born.

"Aren't you interested in seeing where your family is from?" I asked Mike.

"Nah, I can wait until my mom comes to visit us next year. We can go next year with her," he said.

"You sure you want to go on this trip? It's going to cost money to stay at hotels," I said, still conscious that I was not working.

"We wanted to see Japan. Luke and I can take turns driving. We can get lost in all kinds of places. It will be great!" said Mike, the former Explorer Scout.

"*Yaku ba*," I read on the road sign. "I think that means the same as '*shi yaku sho*' in Japanese," I said tentatively. Mike, driving the white Iwakuni MWR van, turned up the small paved road leading to the modern two-story building. We had dropped Luke and Annie off at the orphanage in Kumamoto City and had now, map in hand, been driving around the countryside for over an hour. The road tolls that we paid had amounted to 2,000 yen or about $20.00. We stopped in a parking lot lined with daffodils and narcissus and went inside.

"*Sumimasen*," I said to the Japanese woman in her thirties who worked at the front desk. I missed Annie and her fluent Japanese as I struggled to formulate my sentence. "*Anno . . . watashi wa nikkei desu ga, ima, ojiisan no koseki wo sagashite imasu.*" I told her that I was a foreign-born Japanese and that I was searching for my grandfather's family register. I expected the usual uncomprehending stare that greeted my strange Japanese; instead, the woman smiled and held up her hand.

"*Chotto omachi kudasai, ne. Hamada-san ni tsutae masu.*" She bowed and scurried through a doorway that divided the public area of the city office from what looked like offices and filing cabinets in back. The woman had not thought that I was odd, and she did not seem surprised by my request.

"Hello, I understand that you would like to find your family register," said a slim, clean-cut man in his late twenties. "I am Hamada, I will try to help you."

"You speak perfect English," I said. "Did you study in the United States?"

"No, actually, my father is an American citizen," said Mr. Hamada. "He was born in Honolulu, Hawai'i."

"I'm Mike Nagata and this is my wife Mei. Did you grow up in Hawai'i?" asked Mike, shaking his hand.

"No," sighed Mr. Hamada sadly. "My father's father did not like America and returned to Japan before the World War."

"So you were born in Japan," I said. "But your English is so perfect."

"Yes, my father liked Hawai'i and he liked to speak English, so he has many friends who can speak English," said Mr. Hamada. "He made sure that I studied English in school, and that I took lessons from Americans at *juku* after school."

"Did your father ever return to Hawai'i?" I asked hopefully.

"No, sadly not," said Mr. Hamada. "But perhaps one day he will go to vacation in Waikīkī?" We all smiled. "Now," said Mr. Hamada, "I need documents to connect you to your grandfather. Do you have your father's birth certificate or your grandfather's death certificate?" I rummaged around in my bag and pulled out a manila envelope. Annie and Luke's lawyer, Ms. Urata, had advised us to bring along documentation to prove our connection to Japan.

"I have my father's death certificate, which lists his father's name, and my birth certificate and my passport," I said, handing Mr. Hamada my documents.

"I will take these and be back soon, okay?" he said, giving us a thumbs-up sign. Mike and I smiled and returned his signal. We waited about ten minutes at the counter of the city office. The town of Kamimashiki was green and sparkling clean. Blue green mountain ridges rimmed it on one side and wide rice fields were everywhere. Compared to Tokyo, it was beautiful. I hoped that this was really where my great-grandmother had come from.

Mr. Hamada returned with a wide smile on his face. He read from a sheet of paper he held in his hands. "Your grandfather, Mr. Utaro Matsunaga, died in 1962 on Kopke Street in Kalihi, Honolulu, Hawai'i. " He looked up at me for confirmation. I was stunned. My father's family had indeed lived in Kalihi.

"Yes!" I said. Mr. Hamada then handed me the sheet. He read rapidly, then translated.

"Your grandmother was Mitc. She was his second wife. They had ten children," he announced.

"Yes, my father had nine brothers and sisters, but I didn't know that my grandmother was a second wife," I said.

"Ah," said Mr. Hamada. "The register says your grandfather's first wife divorced him after they had been married one year. They had no children." Our family has never had stories about a first wife. I wondered if the woman divorced my grandfather because she did not want to go to Hawai'i with him.

"Here is your father's name," said Mr. Hamada pointing to one of the ten names listed in *kanji* in vertical boxes printed on the register. My father's name as well as four of the other children's had been crossed out lightly in pencil.

"Why is my father's name crossed out?" I asked. Mr. Hamada looked sad.

"It says in 1941 your father and his brothers refused to be Japanese citizens." That was the beginning of World War II. I had heard that most Japanese men in Hawai'i who held dual citizenship had done the same.

"Ah, I understand," I said. I smiled at Mike, an American military officer. "Our lives are so different now." While we were talking, I noticed that three women and several men who worked in the office had stopped what they were doing and were crowding around us. Mr. Hamada held up the *koseki* sheet and explained rapidly in Japanese that we had found my grandfather's *koseki* and that we were indeed connected to the town of Kamimashiki. The other civil servants in the office smiled broadly at us.

"Where are you going now?" asked Mr. Hamada.

"We need to go back to Kumamoto City to pick up our friends," Mike told him.

"Ah, now we are going to Kumamoto City too to pick up some paperwork," Mr. Hamada said, smiling. "Come and follow our car." He lowered his voice and said in a conspiratorial tone, "We can show you how to avoid the toll roads and arrive at your destination quickly." I watched water-filled rice paddies flash by. One-half hour later, we were in Kumamoto City again without having spent any money on tolls. That night, remembering our ride through the countryside, I wrote: *Graves on hillsides surrounded by paddies, pull in their*

edges to make room for green rice seedlings. Grandparents on hillsides smile with
each rain, as water seeps through ashes and old bones and makes its way down into
the roots of rice plants, to nurture their growth, bringing grandparents closer to a
day when they will caress and nourish their grandchildren again.

Later that week, when Annie and Luke and Mike and I returned to our home at the Tokyo airbase, our taxi drove under the hundreds of cherry trees that lined the base's main street. The trees, which had been brown and bare when we left, were now exploding with pink petals. Addie, who had been fed every day by a neighbor's teenage daughter, seemed happy to see us. I went upstairs to my parents' altar and laid the *koseki* in front of their *o-ihai*. From the window, I could see the sakura blooming as they had in my grandfather and great-grandmother's lives.

That night, I wrote my memories of surviving cancer and a year of chemotherapy in my journal. I had never wanted to write about that year before, but this time, I began the story. Tears rolled down my cheeks when I finished the first paragraph, but I was not unhappy. It was ironic that being surrounded by the cherry blossoms' announcement of new life had somehow allowed me to write about my close brush with death. Again, I had not composed the words that flowed from my pencil onto the pages of my journal. When I reread the images, I could feel the presence of someone that I had always known. Writing had allowed her to blossom in my world. I stared at my parents' *o-ihai* and I thought of my great-grandmother.

New Year's Eve 1991

At a temple in Tachikawa, the night is cold but no wind nips at fingers, face, and ears. We are with friends, other *sansei* from Hawai'i. Uncomfortable, don't know if we really should be here, we are outsiders after all, not really Japanese.

Twelve o'clock:

We enter the temple courtyard through the unpainted wooden gate, walk along the path between cedar trees so tall they must have tasted the same rain as my grandfather, one hundred years ago, when he lived in Japan. A priest standing on the raised platform beside the great temple bell chants a sutra to greet the New Year. His slow syllables float above us as we walk toward him to the center of the courtyard with its bonfire of giant wood beams. A small crowd of Japanese families, the temple's congregation, surrounds the fire; they open their circle and let us in. Their wool coats smell of camphor and incense. The cold of the last midnight of December is at our backs; the orange glow of the fire warms our faces and chests. The night is still. The fire is gentle, flames bloom off the timbers like flowers. Sparks from the tips of the burning logs break off and scatter, rising. Orange sparks that trace commas through the cold gray charcoal air. Hundreds, thousands of chrysanthemum petal sparks. Each is the shape the Japanese give to the soul. Separating, they rise together in a crowd, in a column six feet around. Slow as the sutra being chanted, they float upward. The fire continues burning gently and one group of sparks replaces another. They rise higher and higher, each one still glowing, into the darkness above the tops of the cedar trees.

The black-robed priest pulls the red-and-white silk cords attached to a wooden beam hanging in front of the giant temple bell. Red, the color of blood; white, the color of ashes. One pull, two, three, the beam swings faster and faster, in an arc, a comma, a curve, until wood striking iron booms out round and resonant, the voice of the Buddha, no beginning, no end. Our group in the courtyard exhales in wonder. Our breath is pulled into the river of sparks and rises with them to the treetops. At the priest's invitation, the worshippers begin a single-file procession up the platform stairs. We each bow and take the red-and-white silk cords in hand. We pull wood toward iron. The bell sounds again and again. Concentric rings of sound encircle the bonfire, the people, the giant cedar trees. Each peal rises with the sparks and is replaced by the next, rising higher and higher, carving a warm tunnel of sound, reaching toward heaven.

Ms. Kami

I teach English conversation one night a week at the Matsunaga Electric Company. The only woman in the class is an OL, Office Lady.

"The kanji for my name, 'Kami,' means *paper*," she tells the class sweetly.

"It can also mean biting someone, or being a god," one of the twelve electrical engineers in the class whispers to me.

Ms. Kami is twenty-three years old, unmarried, and in danger of soon being called a "Christmas cake." The Japanese say a Christmas cake is only good on December 25; after that, it is of no use to anyone. So in Japan, a woman who is still unmarried after the age of twenty-five is a "Christmas cake." Ms. Kami is the only woman in her section. She works with twelve engineers, all men. She types, Xeroxes, and answers phones all day, bowing deeply when she answers and again when she transfers calls. Japanese callers can tell even over the phone whether or not a woman's body language is polite. I'm sure Ms. Kami boils the water to keep the teapots full. The women in this company are all hired at eighteen, when they finish high school. All the men are hired at twenty-one when they finish college. Every one.

Ms. Kami has creamy pink-white skin. Her arms and legs are sinewy as the burdock root, which can reach down, as deep as a meter, into the black Tokyo soil. Her cheeks are as red as the sun on Japan's flag. She bicycles to work in all seasons, through summer's heat and typhoon winds and rain, through winter's cold, kerosene-heater haze. She pedals to work six days a week, from her hometown in the suburbs of Tokyo, at least two miles each way.

I think Ms. Kami takes English conversation class because in English, men and women speak to each other in exactly the same way. In Japanese, a woman must address a man by using his family name and the honorary suffix "*-san*." A man may address a woman as "*kimi*," which is the same word he would use to address a child or a dog. In English, Ms. Kami can hold her head up and does not have to bow when she speaks. She is bold as she looks the twelve engineers in the eye and tells of her ambition. "I want to be married. I want to be a powerful mother," she says. She is as tall as most of the men. "She skis in foreign countries," they inform me when she is absent. I think they are afraid of her.

One day, the engineers say, "There is to be a party for you, Sensei, at an old-style Japanese restaurant." I look warily at them. I am American enough to be suspicious.

"I don't eat anything with a head and tail still attached," I say sternly.

"We understand." They smile nervously. The next week, after a quick train trip, we soon sit upstairs in an old restaurant by the train station. We sit on *tatami* mats in a *shoji*-paneled room, our shoes neatly lined up in the corridor outside. We, twelve engineers, Ms. Kami, and I, sit around a long, low table. My students, young college-educated engineers are "New Japanese Men," not the swaggering warriors one might have seen at this kind of restaurant before the Second World War. Respectful of my American sensibilities, they banish the cigarette smokers downstairs. They pour *"ichiban shibori,"* first pressed, cold amber beer into one another's glasses, even though Ms. Kami and I, two women who would usually pour, are in the room.

Soon, tall, empty, amber beer bottles line the table and spill out into the hall with the shoes. Teams of waitresses, securely wrapped and knotted into kimono, run up and down the corridor. Their trays are filled with clinking bottles, bowls of pickles, plates of soybeans, fluffy fried shrimp, and pink *sashimi* rectangles on beds of shredded white daikon.

"Thank you for your patronage," say the waitresses as they bow low, restocking, taking new beer orders at a furious rate. Ms. Kami and I sit at opposite ends of the table. Except that she speaks in Japanese and I in English, we are not so different, two Japanese women speaking with Japanese men. The waitresses are too hurried. They do not notice my speech. The head waitress pulls open the shoji door, and smiles like a *maneki neko*, "good luck cat." "A special surprise to thank you for this party," she says and puts the platter in front of us, then backs out of the room bowing from the waist. On the platter, a silver fish swims in the middle of its own flesh, which has been cut into delicate silver slivers ready for serving. The fish, still alive, flutters toward me through the threads of *daikon* arranged delicately on the plate. I scream, run to the far corner of the room, and put a *zabuton* cushion over my face.

"*Sensei wa kirai desu ka?* Oh, Sensei does not like it?" asks Ms. Kami in surprise. The engineers, horrified, run across the room to stand with me. They watch motionless as Ms. Kami constructs a fort of empty beer bottles to hide the fish. She then flops down beside it and watches entranced. "How active!" she smiles. "So much energy," she giggles. The engineers on my side of the room look on, confused.

"I have heard that this is a special dish," one whispers to me.

"Perhaps we should taste it," suggests another.

"How can you!" I scream at them. They huddle together.

"She does not like it?" Ms. Kami asks, from her end of the table, crinkling her nose, looking puzzled.

"Sensei thinks the fish is suffering," they tell her loftily in Japanese. "Don't sit there watching it," they advise. "Sensei thinks we should feel sorry for the fish!" they scold.

"But it is food," Ms. Kami answers in English. "Of course, it is not a dog or cat," she asserts. "Only food," she shakes her head. Ms. Kami looks wistful. The fish has stopped fluttering. She grabs a half-empty bottle of beer and pours alcohol into the motionless mouth. At my end of the room, the engineers wince as she smiles happily. Hands over their laps, they bow their heads and shuffle behind me. They watch bewitched, as Ms. Kami sits and enjoys the dying spasms of the fish.

"When she is married," they whisper in English above my shoulders, "one must feel sorry for her husband."

Meditation

I walk from my hotel
to the orphanage to see you.
Mt. Unzen's plume of steam
motionless behind me,
in front of me
green morning glory vines climb
up and down wire fences.
I've been thinking
of infants on baby food jars,
innocent smiles on soap boxes,
and I am unprepared
when I see you
for the first time.

Your hair is black
but your face, wrinkled,
uncontrolled muscles grimace.
Your mouth is open and dribbles,
tiny old woman.
Your eyes open,
shine, volcanic stones,
they would glow in moonlight.

I remember Aunty Tanaka
in her dark hospital room,
the priest giving us each
a small blue sponge.
We crowd around her bed.
The green lines of the heart monitors
glowing above us, almost flat.
"They always crave water
before death," the priest tells each of us.
"You will give her an offering,
a last gift of water."

We dip our sponges
in the priest's wooden bowl.
We move toward her pillow,
he's chanting the sutra.
It settles on us heavily
slowing down all our movements.
I don't want to go.
She doesn't move,
she's barely breathing.
Her eyes are dark,
all pupil,
they don't connect with ours.
I'm afraid to touch her,
I hear my heart
and my breathing.
My husband is pushing me
toward her pillow.
I am afraid
as I edge toward the pillow,
she doesn't even know me.
I put my sponge to her open mouth,
smooth water across her wrinkled lips.
She moves her mouth slightly,
relaxes and sighs.
My terror turns to silence,
 the priest is chanting,
"Namu Amida Butsu,"
drawing all suffering toward him,
wrapping it in monotones,
draining it away.

I watch you in your wooden crib,
white sheet wrapped
around your bent, curled body.
They lift you out
and put you into my arms.

They hand me a bottle,
tuck a soft cloth under your chin
and wait
as I stare into your open mouth.
Your gums are wrinkled,
no teeth are showing.
But your lips are the color
of morning glories.
Only fourteen days old,
you know this position,
open wide for the nipple.
I bring it nearer,
touch your lips with white liquid.
You open your mouth wider,
bite hard, furrow your brow
and suckle,
to start the fluid flowing.

"I'm your mother,
I'll take care of you."
I promise into your opaque eyes,
trying to convince you.
You bring your eyebrows together
to frown at me.
You are still suspicious.
Your eyes glitter like obsidian.
You give me a knowing look.
Life is short and uncertain,
you seem to be saying.
Raising your eyebrows like a teacher,
telling me I should remember,
you swallow and sigh.
I watch your throat moving.
You nestle into my body,
forgiving me my ignorance.
The woman may be talking to me.

I can hear only silence.
It condenses into wonder.
I feel the rhythm of your suckling.
We breathe together slowly.
We sing a sutra with these rhythms.
It wraps itself around us,
and drains quietly away.

E David

"E David," I see him only once a year or so and there is something that I need to ask him. He is eight years older than I am, and we only meet at family gatherings. When I was ten, he was eighteen, tall, and tan; he smiled like the sun over the 'Ewa sugar cane fields. He was handsome too, in a mysterious older cousin kind of way. He had the look, like our fathers, brothers, who were, in their 1930s generation, drop-dead, duke 'em up handsome. David and his sister are the first in our family who graduated from college. He is an engineer. He studied the paths of electrons at the university. Maybe hundreds of years ago, he would have been picked to study the paths of stars. Now we are in our fifties and we are at the Willows, sitting at the same table at our Auntie Chiyo's 90th birthday party.

The paper has been full recently of the Rice vs. Cayetano case. The United States Supreme Court ruled that the election for Office of Hawaiian Affairs Trustees, which was limited to voters of Hawaiian ancestry, was unconstitutional. The OHA elections had to be opened to all voters in Hawai'i. Governor Ben Cayetano thinks all voters in Hawai'i should vote. Leaders in the Hawaiian community are split. Some urge only Hawaiians to vote and all others to abstain. Others agree with the governor and hope for a multi-racial turnout. Most of us are confused.

So I say, after we kiss each other hello and exchange the usual "E, howzit? E David, I gotta ask you something," and he with his sunny, radiant, still knock 'em dead even at fifty-nine smile, leans back with good-natured suspicion, narrows his eyes and says, "What?"

"What I going to do about OHA?" I ask. "Should I vote or what?" He looks truly perplexed, as though of all the possible questions I could have asked, he never expected that one.

Then with a Why-the-heck-you-gonna-ask-me-for shrug and a mischievous grin, he purses his lips, leans back in his chair, and offers, "Oh, you asking me? Well, okay . . . you can vote," he whispers with a wink. "It's up to you." I frown at him.

"No joke around," I protest. "I'm not Hawaiian . . . ."

He sighs, then scowls unconvincingly, "No really, you gotta think about everything you know and make up your own mind."

"But you supposed to tell me," I protest. "You graduated from Kamehameha, you graduated from UH, you belong to lots of Hawaiian clubs. Who else I going ask? You *supposed* to tell me," I counter.

"Oh no," he says with a good-natured snort. "I cannot tell you. You gotta think about everything you know and decide." He crosses his arms over his chest. I shoot him an exaggerated frown, but he bites his lips to suppress that blue sky, 'Ewa afternoon grin and I know I will get no further by asking.

So, for the rest of the night, as we go through the buffet line picking up Chinese chicken salad with won ton chips, *lomi* salmon with poi, *pancit* noodles, Japanese green tea *somen* with *tsuyu* dipping sauce, shrimp tempura, Southern fried chicken cutlets, seafood Newburg, Virginia smoked ham, and roast beef, I think about everything I know. I remember riding through the endless sugar cane fields with the slender sword tips of cane leaves waving me to sleep in the back of my father's forest-green 1949 Dodge car heading out to the country to go to David's family's backyard lū'au. It must have been for his Kamehameha graduation, and though I know I must have gone to ones before it, I cannot sort them out in my memory.

Must've been 1959, I remember sitting at a picnic table, top covered with brown wrapping paper, and eating poi out of a paper bowl. I knew even in those days poi was for eating with *kālua* pig fresh out of the *imu* on the side of the house, *lomi* salmon, *limu*, raw *'opihi* and crab, *laulau,* chicken long rice, and sweet onions dipped in red salt, and that I should never, never ask for sugar to be mixed into it. "Who you think you? Baby?" *Kūlolo* was poi in its dessert form, rich with coconut and sugar. I would get it with *haupia,* pineapple, and yellow cake with butter-cream frosting in another plate at the end of the meal. I remember sitting with my Auntie Chiyo and other cousins at a table with a large man who was David's neighbor. The man's hair glistened; I could smell its sweet fragrance. The man watched my Auntie Chiyo closely. She was four feet eleven inches tall and weighed perhaps ninety pounds. She wore a dark dress printed with small white flowers. She looked so different from the other ladies in their bright flowered mu'umu'u. Auntie wore her hair in a bun at the nape of her neck. The other ladies at the lū'au wore their hair loose with flowers pinned over their ears. After observing her for several minutes, the man shook his head. He then leaned over to Auntie and asked with a chuckle, "E Mama, why you no go back Japan?"

People at the table around us grew quiet and, poi in my mouth, black eyes wide in surprise, I watched my auntie and wondered what she would say. Her dark dress made her look even smaller next to the man's bright red-and-green aloha print shirt. But my auntie was a mother who had borne six children, and she surprised me when she looked directly into the man's eyes and said, "I cannot go back Japan, I am Hawai'i born." The man too was surprised at her directness, and grinned. I thought my auntie was going to continue, but just then I remember David in pressed khaki with black ROTC leather belts gleaming, arrived at our table with a large plate of raw white crab.

"Uncle Joe," he said, smiling, "This is my auntie Chiyo, my father's sister." Uncle Joe, accepting the plate of crab, laughed heartily.

"Mits's sister? Oh, you Mits's sister." He looked a little sheepish and proclaimed again, "Hawai'i born eh?"

"Yes," my auntie reiterated, gesturing at the crowd, "we ten children, all Hawai'i born."

I remember other lū'au nights that followed. They must have been for David's brothers' and sisters' graduations, and their weddings. David's mother, my Auntie Ella, was from the Big Island. My older cousins say she was 100% Hawaiian. I have heard, but cannot remember, her maiden name. But that is true for all the rest of my aunties too, except for my mother's and father's sisters; I cannot remember their maiden names either.

David's father worked for 'Ewa Plantation; my father was a mechanic for the Dillingham Corporation. David and his sisters graduated from Kamehameha and the University of Hawai'i. I grew up with my parents' exhortations that I should be like them. He is an engineer. His wife, his Kamehameha school sweetheart, is a bank vice president. His sister and her husband own a business; another sister is married to a minister. A couple of his brothers have moved away from Honolulu. I see them only occasionally at family lū'au time.

I must be frowning as I try to decide what to do because David, who usually drifts away from us girl cousins and our husbands and kids at family parties, is hanging around and having dinner with us at our table. He's usually with the guy cousins who used to go fishing and tell fish stories but now go golfing and compare golf swings. He looks my way and smiles questioningly at me from time to time, but goes back to regaling our table with stories about being bewildered by his daughter who is a stewardess and flies to the Orient several times each month. "No, she cannot get married," he says of his beautiful and eligible offspring, "because then she cannot get free tickets for her mother and father."

I go back to remembering. In addition to plates of food and the sound of conversation and laughter at each 'Ewa lū'au, I remember musicians in aloha shirts, white pants, and white leather shoes singing Hawaiian music. I remember Auntie Chiyo and Uncle Joe talking together over the years, getting older and grayer.

"You get grandchildren? Oh! Great-grandchildren, fast yeah."

As I grew older and began to wear high-heeled shoes, I helped out in the kitchen, cutting up *haupia, kūlolo,* and cakes into little squares and dishing them out onto paper plates. We girl cousins then served the sweets to cousins, uncles, aunties, and neighbors. They smiled at us because our faces, after the years of parties, were familiar. I learned to smile back in spite of the realization that none of them could really remember our names.

"You Tommy's girl? Oh, from Palama yeah?"

But my memories of lū'au are similar to my memories of playing five-card draw on the *lau hala* floor mats of my Uncle Kazu's Kalihi house. I remember the happy smell of his Havana cigar and the red, white and blue poker chips in a circular, carved wooden holder. I remember eating turkey and gravy, *kazunoko, kujira* in miso sauce, deep red sashimi, and drinking orange Nehi soda. We girl cousins learned to run away fast when the boy cousins, including David, played firecrackers. They'd pretend to light and throw firecrackers at us while we screamed and ran from what turned out to be only lighted fuses. All I know is I like the sound of Hawaiian music the way I like the smell of cigar smoke and the color and flavor of orange soda. The liking comes from a well of warm memories that flows from a central source like artesian water. I wonder if it is the same for David.

I always wanted to tell David that I thought he was lucky that he had a mother who was not Japanese ever since that night we visited Uncle Mits in intensive care after his heart attack and I saw Auntie Ella cradling his arm as though it were an infant. She stroked Uncle's head and chest, so that even though he was in a coma, I was sure he could feel her presence. I always envied David and his brothers and sisters who were raised with such open affection and wondered what I would have been like if I had been nurtured that way.

When we finish our food, David, who has survived a heart attack, looks over to the dessert table. I am diabetic and can only watch as he and my daughter go over and fill their plates with guava chiffon cake, tiramisu, and fried *haupia*. They come back and David, with the *kolohe* gusto of a former heart patient on Lipitor, attacks the sweet plateful of forbidden treats. He smiles as he consumes his treasure. I sneak a taste of the sweet white corner of a piece of *haupia* off my daughter's plate.

I know that the Japanese grandfather David and I share spoke Hawaiian he learned when he lived with fishermen in the Diamond Head area after his plantation contract was over. He never learned English, perhaps feeling that struggling to learn one language in addition to his native Japanese was all the concession he would make to his emigration. The odd thing is that while Grandpa knew how to speak Hawaiian, we sit in twenty-first century Hawai'i, and none of us knows how to speak Hawaiian fluently any more. I know because of the reading I have done that teaching children in the Hawaiian language was banned after the 1893 overthrow of Queen Lili'uokalani's government. Without the language, understanding Hawaiian culture even as well as Grandpa did is now for me only a dream.

A smiling young woman of about eighteen approaches our table and waves "Hi" all around before walking on across the room. We all smile at her and as soon as she walks away, look questioningly at each other. My cousin's wife, who is a hairdresser, says, "Florence's granddaughter, from Salt Lake." The rest of us at the table, David; my cousin Grace, a public health nurse; her husband who is a high school principal; and another cousin who is a social worker, all nod in slightly puzzled appreciation. Florence is our cousin, after all; that she has a granddaughter who is a young woman in high heels is quite amazing.

The cousins finish their desserts and I finish my tea. David notices that a few people are walking into the room with bowls of ice cream.

"How they got ice cream?" he whispers. My daughter, who is eight and very alert to anything involving dessert, speaks up.

"Last month when we came here for Mothers' Day, we went to the big buffet table on the other side of the restaurant and got ice cream from the machine," she says. David looks interestedly at the plates. His wife is at work; his daughter is in Tokyo. He is here unchaperoned by cholesterol counters. He realizes the rarity of this opportunity.

"Like go?" I ask. His answer is a slight upward lifting of his chin and a raised eyebrow. So my daughter, David and I slip away from our party cottage and head out into the night on an ice cream quest. We step carefully around the dancing water fountain outside the door and amid palm trees and ferns, sight our objective across the stone-paved courtyard. The central buffet pavilion glows warmly in the night. The ice cream machine is in the far-left corner.

"What if they scold us?" David asks as we walk over.

"We going send the kid first and make her get a bowl." I nod toward my very eager daughter.

"'Kay," David answers and we go in. There are many people in the buffet pavilion and we blend in easily. We take our bowls and line up in front of the soft serve ice cream machine. My daughter goes first and fills her bowl with vanilla, then chocolate. David follows and they both pile hot fudge and chocolate sprinkles over their creations. As we walk back to the party cottage, perhaps it is because David is his mother's son that he notices I am carrying an empty bowl and that I am more thoughtful now than when the night began. He looks pensive then says, "You know, I'm losing track of my sister's family in 'Ewa." I know his sister and her husband still live on his father's land. They have a large family and all the children are now married and parents of their own children. They rarely come to large family gatherings. We walk back to our table in silence. After we are seated, David looks hesitant, and then he asks me a question.

"E, you went Japan and went to see where our family came from?"

"Yep," I answer. "Why?"

He looks a little embarrassed then explains, "See, I play golf with these old guys. You know, Japanese old men, and they say I come from Okinawa." I am mystified. Our family name is a little unusual and difficult to place. It is not the usual Hara, Hara-something, or Something-yama.

"You not Okinawan," I say. "Maybe your friends Okinawan and they want you to be Okinawan too," I reason.

"But we don't come from the main island," David continues. By this time we are back at our table and sitting among the cousins again. "I told the guys we come from an island that is south of the main island, and they said 'Okay, must be Okinawa then.'" I gaze at him and realize that now that our parents have all passed away, I am his only source of information about the Japanese part of his heritage.

"No, we come from the island of Kyushu, from Kumamoto prefecture," I tell him. "There is a river that flows to the left of Kumamoto castle. Grandpa's family must have gotten their name from that river in the Meiji days when commoners were allowed to have family names." As I explain, I am suddenly aware that everyone at our table is listening intently to us.

"Write the kanji for him," says my cousin, who is a nurse.

"Yeah, write down the family name for him," says my cousin the social worker. I realize then that I am the only one at the table who can write Japanese. The others are older than I and were born during or too close to the end of the Second World War when the government closed down all language schools in Hawai'i, and it became a crime to teach all children in any language other than English. I was born after the war hysteria had died down and was able to attend Palama Gakuen, a Japanese language school, in 1956, because litigation to reopen language schools had been filed by the Hawai'i Chinese community. I take out my business card and write the name of the Japanese island, the prefecture, and the town on the back of it. I write our family name in kanji characters with Japanese and English phonetic equivalents. I hand the card to David. He looks at it with satisfaction and puts it in his pocket. He smiles my father's smile.

As we get ready to leave the Willows, we walk toward the exit down a path that is lined with ferns and orchids. As we pass the model of the Hōkūle'a at the Willows's entrance, I realize that David has answered my question about government by talking about family. He comes from a family that has lived in Hawai'i for ten times ten generations. Maybe he is trying to make me realize that it is family that is important. That in Hawai'i it is in spite of government, and because of families that people have been able to survive. So as we say good-bye with a parting kiss on the cheek. I look at him and say, "E David, no good I vote for OHA, but so long as you vote, I think OHA going be okay. No forget though, when you like go back Japan and find the family roots, call me up, 'kay, 'cause I like go with you."

The Safety of Bamboo

"Why do you want your daughter to visit an orphanage?" a friend asked me back home in Hawai'i. "Why did you even tell her she was adopted? Won't you feel broken-hearted when your daughter leaves you to look for a biological mother who didn't raise her?"

At first, I was puzzled by the questions, which seemed illogical because they had been settled in my mind so long ago. I had not thought about them in years. When we were thinking of adopting, I talked to lots of women who were adopted. A lot of them told me the same story, but one woman from the Big Island explained it best. "I had a happy childhood," she said. "I was taller than my sister and I had lighter hair and eyes, but I didn't think I was any different. One day when I was fifteen, my mother took me aside and talked to me about how I was adopted. It was a shock. I felt like I didn't know who I was after she told me. On Monday, I was a yellow hibiscus blooming happily on the same bush as the rest of my family. The next day, I felt cut off from everyone, floating all alone."

My husband and I adopted Roxanne after my friend Annie Ito and her husband Luke adopted Ryan. My husband and I have always known the Itos. Annie and I both attended Palama Japanese School. My husband Mike and Ryan's father Luke attended high school together. Ryan and Roxanne had known each other all of Roxanne's life. Now they were on an airplane, going back to Kumamoto to visit the orphanage that was their first home.

When I first held my baby daughter I remembered the hibiscus story. I wanted my child to always know who she really was, even if it meant that someday she would go looking for her birth mother. I didn't want her to have that feeling of suddenly being alone.

Ryan and Roxanne sat together in the plane. They were less than siblings, or cousins, but more than friends. Ryan was fourteen, but Roxanne was still only twelve. Ryan was 5' 5" tall; Roxanne was three inches shorter. Although Ryan could already chat with his grandmothers in Japanese, Roxanne was just learning and practiced writing hiragana and katakana. Ryan was a piano prodigy while Roxanne played competently. It was obvious that Ryan would always be the leader and Roxanne would always be his cheering section, his follower, his willing accomplice.

Annie and I agreed that we would tell our children that they were adopted from the time that we first brought them home. We also told them that they were from the same orphanage. Perhaps this was the reason that they were always good company for each other. No matter how long they had been apart, they could sit down together and immediately fall into animated conversation, many times finishing each other's sentences. During our nine-hour flight back to Japan, they entertained themselves by watching their chair-mounted screens. They pressed buttons on each other's armrest consoles. They toggled between air speed indicators and a map that showed the distance they had traveled. They played with the electronic menus, watched movies, listened to classical music, popular tunes, and jazz. They checked the hull and cabin temperatures, noting that they were cruising at 500 miles per hour, at 35,000 feet. When they had exhausted all the airline's console options, they delighted in photographing their sleeping fathers' open-mouthed profiles with their digital cameras and playing the pictures back under their ANA airline blankets. Between them, they had already traveled to Disneyland, Disney World, Las Vegas, Alaska, the Eastern Seaboard, and Japan.

"Mom, Ryan wants us to go to Japan with his mom and dad," Rockie had announced six months earlier after reading a message that Ryan sent from his computer to mine. At first, I was cautious. I remembered the party eight years ago when Ry was six and Rockie was four. Ryan and his parents had proudly shown our family the pictures they had taken at the orphanage during a visit to Japan.

"Looks like they had fun," I said that night as Rockie was getting ready for bed. "You want to go to see the orphanage too, Rockie?" My four-year old looked solemn as she crept into the blue nylon sleeping bag, which she insisted on keeping on her bed ever since our camping trip to Bellows Beach.

"What if my birth mother sees me at the orphanage and wants me to go home with her? What if she cries?" Rockie asked.

I bent down to whisper into her ear, "You want to wait a long time so that your birth mother can get over being sad?"

"Yes, that's right," was Rockie's reply.

"Show me the iPod you got for Christmas," Rockie said. Ryan produced his electronic rectangle. "No fair, you got the video one, I still have the one that plays only music," she whined.

"Did you bring the DVDs?" he asked. She dug around in her carry-on luggage.

"Did you bring your DVD player?" She watched with envy as he unzipped the nylon pouch and produced the flat brushed chrome case. "How did you score that?" she asked him.

"Grandma," Ryan said with a mischievous smile as he inclined his head toward his sleeping grandmother.

"Lucky," breathed Rockie. Soon they were laughing uproariously at the antics of black undercover police officers posing as white debutantes. The cabin lights grew dim and Ryan and Rockie fell asleep in their seats. I watched them sleeping like two rumpled puppies. I am an only child and I envy the close connection they have always had. I was glad that we went through with plans for this trip and that Roxanne had decided to see the place where she and Ryan were from.

The children awakened several hours later. We had been in the air for eight hours.

"Look, earthquake," Ryan whispered. Their personal television screens now aired Japanese newscasts. "Fukuoka, that's where the earthquake hit a couple of days ago." He listened carefully to the Japanese narration. "Not much damage, some broken windows. One person died," he reported. They were quiet as they watched the screens. "Fukuoka, that's where we're going, isn't it?"

"We land in Tokyo, then catch another plane to Fukuoka," Ryan's father Luke said. The two friends groaned in unison.

"I hate airplanes!" Roxanne complained. Ryan just sighed. They contented themselves with checking airspeed and altitude gauges as the airplane circled and finally touched down.

Haneda Airport was modern and at first seemed relatively uncrowded. We were loaded onto a small bus, which took us to the main terminal. We were whisked through airport security and ushered into a holding area to wait for our domestic flight to Fukuoka.

"Louis Vuitton! Gucci! Wow, look at the size of that bag," said Ryan.

"Burberry coat, Louis Vuitton bag," countered Rockie. "Do you think all this stuff is real?" she asked.

"Nah, there's a lot of that stuff coming in from China and Korea," scoffed her father. We, the Nagatas and the Itos, public-school educated parents from Palama, looked at each other and shook our heads. Just as mosquito bites and allergy attacks can be unintended consequences of going camping, hypersensitivity to brand names seemed to be an unintended consequence of private school education. The children went on with their international label spotting.

The connecting flight for Fukuoka was called and soon our group was grasping hands to try to stay together as Japanese commuters pressed in around us. The Japanese were all dressed in the same shades of khaki, gray, and black. Rockie's red, white, and gray O'Neill jacket and Ryan's orange Tommy Hilfiger parka stood out in the crowd. Our overcoats looked unusual too: the fabric, the cut, and the colors made the adults in our group easy to spot.

We landed in Fukuoka at nine at night, Japan time, and were whisked aboard a heated touring bus before we had sorted ourselves out. A perky, thirty-something Japanese woman greeted us by speaking into a small microphone.

"I am Izumi, your guide. Welcome to Fukuoka, Japan," she said in near perfect English. "We will go now to your hotel, which is in the old section of Fukuoka City called Hakata. I will be with you for the next seven days of your tour." Ryan and Roxanne sank back into large, deeply upholstered seats, and closed their eyes. "Hakata experienced a 6.0 earthquake several days ago and is still being shaken periodically by aftershocks. I will be in a hotel room on the same floor as yours. If we need to evacuate, I will make sure to knock on your doors," said Izumi-san. We parents were the only ones listening; the children and grandmother were fast asleep.

"Ry has Sharper Image clothes bags that squeeze flat so he can pack lots of clothes. And he has Sharper Image reading lamps that he can clip to his books," Rockie reported to us the next morning. She had been up and visiting in Ryan and his grandmother's room while Mike and I were still trying to convince each other to get out of bed. "When are we going to eat breakfast?" she demanded.

We enjoyed the Miyako Hotel's breakfast buffet, which included a serene presentation of Japanese, German, and American breakfast foods. Early rising hotel guests whispered their appreciation in French, German, Italian, Korean, Chinese, English, and Japanese.

Breakfast was the only time Rockie sat with us; she returned to sitting with Ryan on the tour bus. Rockie and Ryan, the Itos, Mike and I, and Ryan's grandmother made up more than half of our tiny tour group of twelve people. All were from Hawai'i. "Did you sleep well?" asked Izumi-san after the tour group had reassembled on the bus. "I felt some aftershocks last night and was frightened," she revealed. We Hawai'i tourists shook our heads; after twelve hours on two flights, we had slept deeply and felt nothing.

The morning air was crisp and the sky a blue-gray. The buildings of the city were modern high-rises, but they seemed as crowded together as Japanese commuters at the airport did. As I watched the buildings go by, I noticed that windows and doorways seem smaller and more compact than those in Honolulu. The bus driver drove expertly through the streets crowded with cars and rimmed by sidewalks jammed with Japanese commuters rushing to train stations. The bus traveled along the left side of the road and I was glad that I was not driving. Izumi-san remarked that Hakata had been incredibly lucky and suffered almost no damage from the earlier earthquake. As the bus sped smoothly along, Izumi-san explained the history of this part of Fukuoka City. Hakata was the merchant district during the days when the Tokugawa dynasty ruled Japan. Looking out of the windows, I could see nothing that was built before the 1960s. Buildings in the city were fronted by sidewalks but the asphalt of the roadbed seemed to lap at the outer walls of houses and shops as the bus traveled further from the city center. City gave way to brown farmlands as the bus continued its travels. It was March and the grass and trees were still feeling the effects of winter.

"Last week, before the earthquake, Hakata experienced snow!" Izumi-san exclaimed. The bus passed several trees covered in small pink buds.

"*Sakura?*" Annie and I asked hopefully.

"No, not *sakura*, plum blossoms," said Izumi-san. "*Ume*, plum blossoms, usually bloom in February, but this crazy season has confused the trees. The weather is very strange. It is no wonder we had an earthquake." I marveled silently at the idea that the Earth could become confused while the children watched American DVDs, oblivious to the landscape.

"And of course, you must practice. That is the road to perfection. Practice, practice, practice." Ryan scolded in a clipped British accent with Cantonese intonations. Rockie sank back into the upholstered seat giggling as Ryan continued his impersonation of his piano teacher.

The bus stopped at Dazaifu Tenmangu Shrine. "This sect is also known as 'Kotohira jinsha,'" said Izumi-san. My father's family used to go to the Kotohira jinsha temple in Kalihi. A cold spring rain was falling, but we were thrilled with the grove of plum trees at the temple's entrance. Annie, Grandma, and I walked from one tree to the next marveling at the pink cloud of flower petals bursting from brown branches. Mike and Luke pulled out new digital cameras and fumbled with focus buttons while struggling to hold umbrellas over our heads. Shutters clicked and bulbs flashed as family groups were posed under trees covered with clouds of blossoms in all imaginable shades from deep magenta to a pink so delicate it was almost white. We made a quick trip to the temple for a bath in incense smoke, a run down the main shopping street for folk crafts, and a bathroom stop before sprinting once again onto the beautifully heated bus. I was surprised at how fast Ryan's grandmother, shod in SAS lace-ups, could travel.

"Japan is a country of details," intoned Izumi-san as the bus motored forward toward the mountain town of Hita Mameda. "Now, four in twenty public toilets are Western-style, and there is a special button in each stall that you can press to play the sound of a toilet flushing so that no one needs to be embarrassed that the person in the neighboring stall can hear an inappropriate sound."

"Japan is a country of details but not hot water," whispered Annie as she passed me a bottle of hand lotion. My hands were still pink and tingling from the rest stop's ice-cold tap water.

Small mountain towns flashed by: each town was basically the same. At the edge of each cluster of houses, there was a hill on which a bamboo forest climbed the slopes on one side, while cedar trees descended toward rice paddies down the other.

"The Japanese say that a bamboo forest is the safest place to be during an earthquake," said Izumi-san, perhaps still remembering the aftershocks in Hakata. "The roots of the bamboo grow underground to form a thick network. The roots hold the earth firmly in place so no giant cracks can open. The bamboo has so many uses in Japanese life. The Japanese people use bamboo and cedar for building material." Our tour group gazed out at the landscape. Flooded rice fields stretched across the land. Many in our group had grandfathers who had been rice farmers.

Back on the bus, we began the ascent toward Mount Aso National Park. Izumi-san was back on the microphone again. "Send us your young people," she said. "Japan is becoming an old country. There are more old people now and no young people to take their places. Young Japanese women do not want to marry and live with mothers-in-law and raise babies anymore. Soon, there will be no young workers to support the country. The situation is very serious," she concluded. Annie and I looked protectively at our son and daughter. We felt a tiny twinge of guilt but knew we would never send the children back.

"Look, snow," Ryan breathed. Rockie, who had been playing intently with Ryan's Gameboy, looked out of the window. Sure enough, light flurries were falling around the bus. There was a dusting of snow on the ground as the bus, engine roaring, climbed winding roads toward a pass through the mountains. A light covering of snow decorated fence posts and boulders as the bus began to descend through bare, brown pastureland. Soon, it pulled in to a rest stop that looked like a Swiss chalet. The group descended and rushed to the restroom facilities, then into the country store as quickly as possible to escape the cold. Ryan and Roxanne hurried around to sample all of the sweets and cookies that were set out next to stacks of boxes.

"The chocolate *mochi* is good, Mommy," Roxanne said, "and the choco bits are good too." Ryan was looking at Japanese name stamps and reading the hiragana to find his name, Teruo. Roxanne joined him to look for her name, Mitsue. Soon however, Roxanne was distracted by a soft stuffed animal that was not a calf, not a piglet, not a puppy, but had features that could have belonged to any one of those baby animals.

"What's that?" I asked as Roxanne carried it around the store.

"A Japanese hamster," she said confidently. "Can we buy it?"

"You have twenty stuffed animals on your shelf at home and five more on your bed," I pointed out.

"He can sleep on my bed at home with SpongeBob, Piglet, Girl Scout Bear, and me," Roxanne said. "His name is Hammie." I sighed my usual sigh, then pulled out three one thousand yen bills. Back on the bus, heading downhill toward Kumamoto City, Roxanne fell asleep cradling the hamster. I wondered if she was feeling anxious about visiting an orphanage that she did not remember.

The New Otani Kumamoto shone with mirrored glass and marble floors and counters. The rooms were small but warm and comfortable. Mike and Luke, chatting animatedly about Coverdale college funds and retirement accounts, took Ryan's grandmother and the children to see the train station and its underground network of food booths next to the hotel. Annie and I stayed in the hotel coffee shop to chat about the next day's visit to the orphanage.

"I wrote to the orphanage directress, Mrs. Shigemura, in November," Annie began. "A Mr. Ogawa wrote back to say that Shigemura-san is now an administrator in the Kumamoto Prefecture government office and that he is now in charge of the orphanage."

"Have you been sending donations and letters every year to the orphanage?" I asked shyly, sure that the answer would be yes.

"No, we used to send a donation and Ry's picture once a year, but we haven't sent anything for a long, long time," whispered Annie. I smiled in surprise.

"We haven't sent anything since pre-school either. I guess as time went on, we didn't want to share her with anyone else," I confessed with relief. We sat together in silence. I remembered baths in sinks, diaper rashes, runny noses, scraped knees, first days at school, tears that were hugged away, visits to emergency rooms, colds overcome, school awards, and piano recitals—*tsunagari*—small filaments that tie mother and child, father and child, mother and father, together. Over the years, like the roots of a bamboo forest, these small filaments bound our family together.

"Even so, Mr. Ogawa has offered to come to the hotel to pick us up tomorrow morning," Annie continued. "We can tell Izumi-san that we will miss tomorrow's tour of Kumamoto Castle and Suizenji Park."

"Don't unwrap my hotel toothbrush and toothpaste," Roxanne instructed me in our hotel room that night. "I'm using the ones I got from the first hotel and saving all the other ones to take home."

"Are you going to give them away to your friends?" I asked hopefully.

"Of course not," sniffed Rockie. "Here's my list of people I'm going to buy Doctor Grip pens for," she said as she waved a piece of paper in my direction.

"Why don't you just buy them pens from Longs Drugs at home?" I asked. "We have Pilot pens in Hawai'i, you know." Rockie rolled her eyes.

"No, the kind they have here are better!" she insisted. "They have shaky Doctor Grips, perfumed Dr. Grips, and all different colors here," Rockie intoned with authority. I sighed. The world of twelve-year-old girls was full of subtle and mystifying distinctions. Rockie continued working on her list, crossing off and adding names. "Tina likes purple, Nicole likes blue . . . I think Donna is my best friend so I can buy her a shaky Dr. Grip with chimes." Satisfied at last, she stowed her list in her backpack.

"Daddy, you ate the *shu* crème we bought at the train station," she wailed as she searched in her bag.

"Not," her father replied innocently. "And anyway, I checked first and it didn't have your name on it," he teased as I left them to their usual argument and headed for the tiny hotel bathroom.

Mike was snoring peacefully and the room was dark when I emerged from my long, luxurious soak in a porcelain tub. "Mom," Rockie whispered as I passed by her bed.

"Yes," I whispered back.

"When we go to the orphanage tomorrow, will they let me look at my file?" Rockie asked softly. I had wondered when she would ask about the file that might contain information about her birth mother. I had wondered about it many times myself.

"I don't know," I answered truthfully. When Mike and I first took Roxanne home twelve years ago, the orphanage directress told us that the orphanage kept a file on each adoptee. Adoptive families were encouraged to write letters and send pictures to be placed in the file. Birth mothers sometimes came back to look at the contents of the files, she had said.

"Ryan's mother said Mr. Nagata's son went back to look at his file," I told her, "but he was already twenty-one and had finished college when he went back."

"He was the first Hawai'i boy that was adopted from the orphanage," Rockie whispered gravely. "Did he find his birth mother?" she asked.

"I don't know, I don't think so, or Auntie Annie would have told us," I said.

"Ryan said he didn't see a file cabinet when they went back a long time ago," Rockie said sleepily, cradling Hammie the Japanese hamster. She turned over and was soon asleep. I lay in bed for some time, wondering if the tearful young woman I had spoken with twelve years earlier had indeed come back to see pictures of the baby she had given up. I prayed that she had been able to begin again and that she was now sleeping in a house surrounded by a husband and children.

The next morning, over breakfast, the adults conferred over the monetary gifts we would give to the orphanage. Rockie and Ryan sat at their own table eating bacon, eggs, ham, and hash browns from the American breakfast buffet, chatting animatedly. They did not seem nervous about revisiting their first home. After breakfast, Mr. Ogawa, a fiftyish, balding man who spoke accented English, picked us up in a white Toyota van. "*Ohayo gozaimasu*," we greeted him in Japanese.

"Yes, good morning, everyone," Mr. Ogawa replied in English, reaching out to shake our hands instead of bowing. Parents, children, and grandmother climbed in for the ride through Kumamoto City traffic to the orphanage.

"The *ume* is blooming," Ryan's mother said as we pulled into the orphanage parking lot. We looked over the small garden in front of the administration cottage as we piled out of the van. Daffodils, tulips, and colorful decorative cabbages also bloomed in the tiny garden. "I remember *sakura* when we came to pick up Ryan," Annie said nostalgically.

"I remember sunflowers," I said as I reached for Roxanne's coat sleeve. I was suddenly aware that at twelve, she was now the same height as I was. The last time I had been in this garden, she had been an infant wrapped from head to toe in 100% cotton, asleep in my arms. The families stood at the door of the administration cottage taking pictures of one another. "We have to put these in the scrapbook alongside the pictures we took twelve years ago," I said.

"Look, a pony!" Roxanne exclaimed excitedly. She and Ryan trotted off across the yard to the pony's tiny stall. Several young Japanese boys were grooming the small animal. Rockie and Ryan stopped shyly a short distance away from them, and both groups watched the other in interested silence.

"Please come inside for some tea first," Mr. Ogawa called and Rockie and Ryan came reluctantly back to the administration cottage.

"*Arigato gozaimasu, samui desu nei*," Annie thanked him.

"Please sit and have some tea first," Mr. Ogawa replied, again declining to answer in Japanese. Inside the sunny office, we were seated in a tiny conference area in front of Mr. Ogawa's desk. Instead of the usual green tea, a young woman served us black English tea in china cups with saucers. The young woman, who was probably called an OL, office lady, offered everyone straws filled with sugar and cream sealed in tiny individual plastic thimbles. Rockie and Ryan each took a shortbread cookie shaped like a thistle from a china plate that had been set on the coffee table in the midst of the circle of chairs. I wondered if the children were scanning the room looking for file cabinets. "Ah . . . the children have grown very tall," said Mr. Ogawa beaming at Ryan and Rockie from behind his desk.

"Ryan plays cello in Honolulu's Junior Symphony Orchestra," I said proudly. "He has been playing the piano since kindergarten too."

"Roxanne swims for her school in competitions," Annie pointed out. "She also has been playing the piano since kindergarten." Annie and I, who would never have boasted about our own children, bragged shamelessly about each other's kids.

"Yes," said Mr. Ogawa, showing the group a stack of letters and photographs, "many, many of our children have good lives in American and Europe." The phone on his desk rang and after a short conversation, he said, "One of our staff who was here when the children were first adopted has come out of retirement to see them. Will you come with me to the Baby House where she is waiting to meet them?" Rockie and Ryan walked together and continued looking carefully around the administration cottage on their way out.

Pulling on our coats, our group accompanied Mr. Ogawa out across the compound toward the Baby House. We walked through the Administration Cottage's garden, crossed a sandy ball field, and walked into the grassy play yard of the Baby House. It was a modern wooden building with sliding glass doors. A group of children who looked to be about three to four years old played outside. There were more children than I remembered from my visit twelve years before. A small boy turned our way and I stared at him in surprise. Luke had seen him too.

"That kid looks exactly like Ryan did when he was four," his dad whispered.

"We have a picture of him that looks exactly like that," I agreed.

"Hey Ry, that kid looks just like you when you were three," his father said softly. Ryan said nothing, but Roxanne snapped a picture of the group of children with her digital camera.

"Mom, we have a picture of that shoebox in my baby album," Rockie said as we took off our shoes on the Baby House's sunny porch. We carefully arranged our shoes next to the yellow shoebox that held twenty pairs of tiny sneakers.

"*Irrashaimase*," we were greeted by three of the five women who worked in the Baby House. The women wore brightly colored aprons or housewives' smocks. They bloomed like plum blossoms in the clean, large interior space. The walls were unpainted and looked like natural wood; the floor was also made of smoothly finished wood planks. There were two circular pits in the floor about twelve inches deep and five feet across; these were lined and carpeted with a thick gray rug. I remembered sitting at the edge of one of these pits, my legs dangling down into the carpeted bottom, holding Rockie in my lap for the first time. Today, we watched little ones first learning to stand pull themselves up against the sides of the pits. The circles served as safe, soft playpens for several toddlers at a time.

"*Ah, ookiku natta nei!*" crooned a motherly woman who rushed up to Rockie and Ryan. Mr. Ogawa smiled as he introduced her.

"Of course you do not remember Mrs. Nakasone," he said to Rockie and Ryan, "but she took care of you when you were babies here." Mrs. Nakasone caressed each child's arm.

"Oh, you are so tall now!" she said happily in Japanese. Ryan and Rockie shot each other embarrassed looks but smiled back at her. Annie and I looked at each other uncomfortably. Since we did not know that Mrs. Nakasone would be here, neither of us had brought *omiyage* gifts for her. Grandma Ito, who had been watching from the fringe of the group, reached into her large leather handbag and pulled out a box of Ed and Don's chocolate-covered macadamia nuts. She bowed to Mrs. Nakasone and handed her the gift.

"*Osewa ni narimashita,*" she said, bowing gently. Mrs. Nakasone smiled delightedly. Annie and I smiled at Grandma in gratitude. Grandma Ito beamed back benignly.

I looked around at the room I had last visited twelve years ago. "Here's the sink that Mrs. Nakasone showed me how to bathe you in," I exclaimed. The party walked across the room to two sinks set into smooth imitation marble countertops.

"And here is the same crib I first saw you in," said Annie as she lovingly caressed the worn bars of one of seven plain wooden cribs in an adjoining room.

"Stand over here and let us take before and after pictures!" Annie and I exclaimed to the children.

"Oh, come on Mom, how do you know it's the exact same one?" Ryan said suspiciously. The children both made lemony faces but walked slowly over to stand next to cribs that they remembered only from pictures in their baby albums. Mike and Luke snapped away on digital cameras, memorializing the moment.

The children walked back to the center of the large, wood-paneled room and were greeted by three young women carrying babies, who appeared to be about six months old. I counted five babies in this group, the youngest about six months and the oldest about one year. The three women caring for this clutch of infants were spreading tiny futon quilts on the smooth wooden floors. Suddenly, one woman, about twenty-something, with ruddy pink cheeks and hair tied back in a ponytail, handed Roxanne one of the two infants she was carrying. "Nē-chan will carry you for awhile, Shin-chan," she said in

Japanese. She called Roxanne "big sister" in Japanese and had entrusted my twelve year old with a six-month-old infant. Roxanne opened her eyes wide in surprise. This was the first baby she had ever held in her arms. Shin-chan stared at her for a moment, then snuggled into her soft, warm O'Neill jacket. Another young woman, who was also carrying two infants, smiled mischievously and plopped one of them into Ryan's arms. This baby too stared wide-eyed at Ryan's orange jacket and snuggled in happily. The two Hawai'i children looked at each other incredulously, then at their mothers, hoping to be rescued. Annie and I just smiled as their dads snapped away with the digital cameras. The three caretakers, each with another baby on one hip, were busy trying to maintain their feeding schedules and left for the kitchen to fetch bottles and clean diapers. They returned and handed Rockie and Ryan each a bottle of formula. Annie and I helped the children adjust the babies' heads to comfortable positions for feeding, then stepped back to savor the sight of our half-grown children taking a long step toward adulthood. The babies' three caretakers seemed grateful for the extra hands and used the time to set five quilts on the floor, then feed and burp the other three babies in their care. Roxanne watched Shin-chan drink the contents of his bottle with big sisterly pride.

"When will Shin-chan go home with his new mother and father and get his own room and his dog?" she smilingly asked Mr. Ogawa.

"Well, Miss Mitsue," he answered, using her Japanese name, "Japan is now a different country. Have you heard that we have the most rapidly aging population in the world?" He looked grave and had stopped smiling.

"We heard something about that on the tour bus," said Ryan's father.

"Ah yes," Mr. Ogawa continued, "so in 1994, the Japanese government changed the law, to keep children inside the country. Although these children, Mitsue and Teruo, and many others found homes outside Japan until 1994, since then, it is almost impossible for foreign people to adopt Japanese babies."

"But Japanese people can still adopt them," said Ryan, looking down at the baby he was feeding.

"Yes, of course," said Mr. Ogawa, "but Japanese people are very cautious about the babies they will adopt. Usually, they will adopt only one that is born in their own family."

"Then what will happen, to Shin-chan?" asked Roxanne, who was suddenly holding her baby closer to her chest. "How will he grow up and go to school?"

"This baby is lucky," said Mr. Ogawa. "He has a brother here too. His mother left his brother with us about five years ago and this year she came back with another baby." Annie and I and Grandma Ito looked at each other sadly. We had been looking at the faces of the other babies in the room. Some were dark and small, others had lighter hair and eyes. All of them were very beautiful.

Roxanne stared intently at Shin-chan's face. He had fair, almost translucent skin like hers, and his long eyelashes almost brushed his cheeks. He was drinking his milk intently. I gazed at him too, remembering Roxanne's face when she was six months old. This baby could easily have been her brother. Annie and Luke gazed out the window toward the three year old playing outside who looked so much like their son that he could be a younger sibling. I shuddered as I realized that we had been incredibly lucky to be working in Japan at just the right time to be able to adopt our children with none of the current problems.

"Can we send Shin-chan toys for Christmas?" Roxanne asked, seeking a way to remain close to him.

"Well," I answered, "we can send some toys, but all of the children own all the toys together."

"But he should have a Hammie and SpongeBob and Bear of his own," Rockie insisted, as her eyes filled with tears.

"The children will stay in the Baby House until they are four years old," Mr. Ogawa continued. "They will then go and live in cottages with their cottage parents and many brothers and sisters of different ages. This is a children's and an old people's home. The children learn to take care of each other, and they visit the old people and help care for them too. We all live together and help each other."

"How long will they stay?" asked Ryan.

"Until they are eighteen. Then they usually leave to find a job."

"What if they want to go to college?" asked Mike.

"Of course, if a child wants to go to college, we will help him find money and allow him to go," Mr. Ogawa said.

"How many children have you sent to college?" asked Luke.

"No one," said Mr. Ogawa softly. "When they become eighteen, they want to move out and begin their own lives." The caretakers had fed and burped their three babies and had laid each one on a quilt on the floor. A rosy-cheeked caregiver in a pink apron came back to Roxanne and reached for Shin-chan. Roxanne, who was so startled to receive him thirty minutes ago, now seemed reluctant to give him back.

"You must give him back, Nē-chan," the woman said with a smile. "This one always spits up a lot of milk after he drinks."

"Give him back, he's gonna spew!" Ryan translated urgently and Roxanne quickly handed Shin-chan back. The caretaker put him down on his little quilt and sure enough, a small geyser of milk emerged from his plum petal lips and soaked into the cotton cloth. The women giggled and quickly put a dry quilt beneath Shin-chan, who smiled happily and settled into a nap. The women left to help tend to another group of two year olds at the opposite end of the room. Five children were sitting in tiny chairs with tables attached. The children were clamoring for the miso soup and rice that was being ladled into small wooden bowls. Roxanne, Ryan, and Mrs. Nakasone stayed with the five infants contentedly sleeping on their quilts. The children stroked the infants' backs from time to time, lost in their own separate thoughts.

Back in the white orphanage van, Ryan and Roxanne were quiet as they replayed the photographs that we had taken of the orphanage with our digital cameras. I wondered how long the children would remember what they had seen. I wondered if Rockie would ask me about the filing cabinets they could not find.

"So now you know where the place is," said Mike as Mr. Ogawa drove the van back to the hotel.

"You can come back and find it if you need to," Ryan's father added. I listened expectantly, waiting for the children to comment, but they only huddled closer together to view the pictures on each of the four cameras.

"Did you have fun learning to be big sisters and brothers?" Annie asked. Again, neither of the children responded as they continued to look at the pictures in our cameras. We rode on in silence until the van passed through downtown Kumamoto City. Ryan then began reading the katakana signs displayed along the sides of buildings,

"Unikulo—Unique Clothes?" he speculated. "Euro-Kutto, Euro-Dezainu—European Cut and European Design?" he said as Annie and I looked at him with puzzled expressions on our faces. "Izumi-san told me that her brother likes those clothes. Can we go to that store?" he pleaded. "Dokuta Gurippu—Doctor Grips? Is that building Mitsukoshi Department store?" he asked.

Roxanne, who had been listening to Ryan intently, chimed in, "Oh Mom, we need to get some of those shaky Doctor Grip pens for all my friends. My friend Jenna brought me one for Christmas last year. They're so cool!" I wondered why the children refused to say anything about the orphanage. I wished that they were toddlers again so that we could snatch them up in our arms and tickle them until they answered our questions. As I watched them, I knew that it was too late. They were uniting against us, digging in their heels. They had discovered their independence and were insisting on dealing with their feelings in their own way. I wondered if this was how they retreated toward safety, just as the Japanese during earthquakes retreat into the safety of bamboo.

Signs

We get into my Saturn. I am driving you to swim practice. On Judd Street, we pass the sign, *Watch for the Blind*. It inevitably sets off a chain of thoughts in my head that is as irresistible as slipping off my sandals so that I can drive barefoot. The phrases roll forward in my mind: *Watch for the Blind, Listen for the Deaf, Speak for the Mute, Walk for the Paralyzed*. Halfway down Judd Street, they begin to decompose slightly. *Deduce for the Clueless, Sniff for the Scentless, Taste for the Tasteless, Decide for the Wavering, Ignore the Ignorant*. They continue until I reach the stop sign at the corner of Nuʻuanu and Judd, where I can see the cemetery where my grandparents are buried. *Live for the Dead*.

Watch for the Blind. I peek at you out of the corner of my eye. You've released the seat back and are comfortably stretched out, feet under the dashboard, head below the window. This year you are taller than I am. You have your bathing suit on under a Roxy T-shirt and board shorts. Your thick black hair is gathered into a Gummi elastic band and looped back on itself. You have headphones over your ears, like Michael Phelps, and have closed your eyes to block out the world. After a year of daily swim lessons, you compete against other girls your age who can cut through water like sunlight. This is your afternoon swim practice attire. Each morning, you wear a uniform and attend a private girls' school, which was founded in the nineteenth century by a woman. Your music bag, containing your piano practice books, lies under the car's seat. Musical notes run in wave-patterned arpeggios over their pages. You have studied piano for the past three years and this summer you played in a white gown on the stage of the concert hall, during a mass recital, one of a hundred students of the best piano teachers. I hope that this is what your birth mother had in mind. "Make her an American girl," she said. I gaze at you and wonder if she would think that I have followed her instructions.

You looked unfinished when I first saw you. You were fourteen days old and your skin was still almost transparent. I could see the network of blue veins and red arteries beneath it. Your hair was black and stuck up in tiny wisps. Your eyelashes were so long they reached down your cheeks. You were round and sturdy. You opened your mouth to cry and I could see your gums, which were wrinkled and pink without any teeth. The Baby House directress, Mrs. Nakasone, picked you up and put you in my arms. I tensed up expectantly and rearranged my arms to support your head. You knew you were being lifted; you shifted your body in puzzlement. You felt the warmth of my chest; you heard my heart. You snuggled in toward the warmth, the sound. You knew how to find safety; you knew how to struggle toward love.

You are adopted but you were never abandoned. Your birth mother was a woman who knew about medicine. She knew that the first milk to flow from a mother's breasts would confer upon an infant a lifetime of protection. I know that she insisted that her infant suckle from her breasts even though she was warned that this would forge a painful connection that would pull at her forever. That first drink of clear liquid was an irreplaceable legacy, a push toward excellence. I often wonder if your birth mother imagines you now though she has not seen you for twelve years.

Listen for the Deaf. My father once told me that our family name came from a river in Japan. But my father loved to exaggerate about the fish, the big waves, the former girlfriends he used to catch. He used to tell young apprentices to "Quick, quick, go bring me one bucket of steam!" and chuckle as they searched frantically around the auto shop. He used to tell lots of stories, so I never listened when he talked about how our family got its name because I never knew if I could believe him. Before I married, people I met asked about my family's name. Is it Malaysian? Indian? Samoan? There was always the inevitable question, "Are you sure it's Japanese?" It was a relief when I married, because my husband's name, Hara, is like Smith in America. It is unquestionably a Japanese name. When I went to the orphanage in Kumamoto to claim you, the directress asked me many questions. "Why do you want a Japanese baby?" "What does your mother-in-law think of adoption?" "Where is your husband's family from?" I answered all these as she nodded, her mouth pursed seriously. Then she asked me the tough one: "What is your maiden name?" I answered, prepared for her narrowed stare. "Oh," she smiled. "Of course your family is from Kumamoto." I was surprised. She had claimed me.

"How do you know we are Kumamoto-ken?" I asked.

"Two rivers flow across Kumamoto," she answered. "Kumamoto Castle is built between them. One is Tsuboigawa, the other river has your family's name."

Speak for the Mute. Your birth mother walked slowly into the directress's office. I was amazed at how beautiful she looked. Though she kept her head down modestly, she moved confidently as though she had grown up playing athletic games. She sat in a chair opposite me. She looked then as you are

163

beginning to look now. She had long eyelashes and skin as fair as the chin of a white peach. In my broken Japanese, I asked why she did not keep you. "My boyfriend and I were together for two years," she explained in a soft voice. "When I became pregnant, I had no doubt that we would marry and keep the child. But when I told him," she paused and looked down at the carpet, "when I told him, he said that this was not his child. My father and I went to talk with my boyfriend's family," she went on. "We explained that I had only one boyfriend, that this could only be his baby. We begged them," she concluded. I waited for her to continue, but she just sat and looked at her hands silently. The directress of the orphanage continued the story.

"This girl and her father tried everything they could, but the boy and especially his mother continued to deny that he had anything to do with the child. They turned their backs on this girl and asked her to leave their house." We three women, your birth mother, the directress, and I, sat silently in her office. Finally, your birth mother raised her head and spoke. "In Japan, we all have a *koseki*." She looked toward the directress to explain the word.

"*Koseki* is a birth record. It lists the person's mother and father and all of the brothers and sisters in the family," the directress explained as though she had explained many times before.

"Yes, birth record," your birth mother went on. "When we in Japan try to go to school, go to university, get a job, or get married, we must show this *koseki* so everyone . . ." She brought her palms together as though she was holding a book. She stopped again and looked troubled.

"Oh," I picked up where she had left off, "so if this child's *koseki* has no father's name, she cannot go to school and get a good job . . . I see."

"If the child is adopted," the directress added, "it is given a new *koseki* with you and your husband listed as father and mother."

"And then she can do anything she wants," I marveled. Your birth mother looked at me and smiled. "In America, we have no *koseki*. We only show our own school records and letters of recommendation from our teachers to get a job," I told her.

"Make her an American," she said.

When I told this story to my English conversation class back in Tokyo, the electronics company engineers who were handing around your first pictures with their nicotine-stained fingers looked thoughtful. They glanced furtively at each other until the section chief cleared his throat.

"These women have not told you the entire truth," he said in English. The others nodded slightly.

"What do you mean?" I said, my English allowing me to speak more directly than a woman ever could in Japanese. "Why would they hide anything?"

"You see," the section leader said, looking uncomfortable, "Japan is a man's country. What I mean is, there are many men who have babies with women who are not their wives."

"So there are many children who cannot live full lives?" I asked.

"No, the child does not suffer just because the man is not married to the woman," he said, moving his fingers nervously as though searching for a packet of cigarettes.

"I don't understand," I said, full of a foreigner's inquisitiveness. "Why did my baby's birth mother say the baby couldn't go to good schools or have a good job?"

"In Japan," the section leader began, then paused to brush his fingers over his lips, "in Japan, a man can register a child into his *koseki*, even if he is not married to its mother." He smiled self-consciously.

"Can't a mother register a child into HER *koseki* too?" I asked, wide-eyed. The engineers all shifted uncomfortably in their chairs. They were not used to so much frank conversation.

"If a woman registers a child into her *koseki*, then the child is illegitimate and both mother and child will face many problems," the section chief explained apologetically. I scanned the slightly embarrassed faces of the engineers I had taught for the past three years.

"You mean even in this century, it is only a man's word that can make a child fully legitimate?" I asked with genuine American disbelief.

"Of course, this is Japan," the section chief answered gently.

Deduce for the Clueless. The directress of the orphanage said that both my husband and I had to be present before we could take you home. My husband was in Korea on business so I had to make arrangements to return again the next week. In the meantime, Mrs. Nakasone, the Baby House directress, showed me how to wash your bottles and make your formula. "You must wash the bottles, nipples, collars, and caps in soap and water," she said in clear, Tokyo-accented Japanese. I smiled because earlier I had heard her use Kumamoto-ben, the odd colloquial language of this area, to the Baby House staff. "Then you must rinse each bottle with clear water seven times. It is very important to remove all traces of soap." I nodded and took notes in English on my little notebook. "You can then fill the bottles with boiled water. Then put the bottles in your traveling bag." Mrs. Nakasone showed me how to measure the powdered Japanese formula into a plastic container with five sections for easy storage of a full day's milk supply. "You mix the powder with the water just before you feed the baby," she said. As Mrs. Nakasone and I looked down at you sleeping in your tiny wooden crib, she said, "When you put her to sleep, lay her on her side. Roll up two small blankets and place one along her back, and one along her stomach so that she cannot roll over on her back or on her stomach." I noticed that you were indeed sleeping on your side.

"Is it because you don't want the back of her head to become flat?" I asked.

"No," Mrs. Nakasone answered, looking at me strangely. "American scientists who study babies who stop breathing think that putting them to sleep on their stomachs is a bad idea; they may smother against the mattress. Japanese scientists, on the other hand, think that babies sleeping on their backs might choke if they spit up milk in the night. We here at the Baby House, advise you to put the baby to sleep on its side." I wrote everything down. I wanted to make no mistakes. "When you come back," Mrs. Nakasone continued, "bring baby diapers for the trip home, two sets of undershirts, two top shirts, stockings, and a baby blanket, all cotton. Make sure everything is cotton, 100%," she cautioned. I wrote this too in my tiny notebook and wondered if I could find everything in time.

Taste for the Tasteless. I spent the night at the Green Hotel. An orphanage staff member drove me there in the institutional van and helped me register. I rode the tiny elevator alone upstairs to my tiny room. The room had a double bed and a closet-sized bathroom with a clean toilet and shower. I peered out the one window, which overlooked the clean, modern street below. In the dusk, I could see many women rushing home. They stopped in at a small store across the street and emerged with groceries in white plastic sacks. Beyond the store was the small side road that led to the orphanage. I could not see the buildings, which were hidden by trees. I stared in the direction of the Baby House. I remembered the warmth and weight of you in my arms. Could I become your mother? Could I bond with you so completely that I would willingly jump in front of a bus if I knew it could save your life? Your birth mother's face surfaced in my memory. I was forty-three years old. I could have easily been your mother's mother. Was I too old? Did I know what I was doing? The street became darker and darker. The streetlights came on with a yellow glow. I realized that I was hungry.

The little grocery story across the street was clean and smelled of vegetables and sugary soy sauce. Servings of food sat on counters in small foam trays covered with clear plastic wrap. I chose crab and potato croquettes and sticky rice cooked with mountain vegetables. I stared in wonder at *mochi* wrapped in brine-pickled cherry leaves. Other pieces of *mochi* were decorated with sticky grains of sweet rice colored in brilliant pinks and greens. I had not seen *mochi* like this since I was seven. I remembered sharing pieces of these sweet, chewy desserts with my grandparents, who were immigrants from Kumamoto. Standing in the grocery store, I felt that I could go into the past and snatch some treasures from my childhood. I bought my dinner and headed back to my hotel.

I had eaten the crisp croquettes and the mountain vegetables steamed in sticky shoyu-seasoned rice. I was savoring the thought of returning to my grandparents' kitchen when I ate my dessert. I lifted the white *mochi* and traced the brilliant pink camellia made of individual rice grains with my tongue. I was just about to bite down when a slamming door and laughing voices seeped through my wall from the next room. I listened and thought I heard a man and woman's voices. The wall was embarrassingly thin and not at all soundproof. As I ate my *mochi*, I found myself trying to picture the happy couple next door. Were they a husband and wife trying to escape their children and in-laws? Were they colleagues from a company who had gone away for a romantic weekend? Were they college students from Kumamoto University playing at being adults? The sound of laughter died away and, to my chagrin, was replaced by occasional moans of passion. I contemplated the last pink *mochi* wrapped in a brine-soaked cherry leaf. The salty and sweet flavors mingled in my mouth as I bit into it. I remembered the grief on your birth mother's face as she asked me to take her baby to America. I hoped the couple next door had taken precautions against an unwanted pregnancy. If I could hear them, they would probably be able to hear me if I called out, "*Abunai yo, ki wo tsukete ne. Big pilikia ni naranai yoo ni*," using three languages simultaneously. "Danger, be careful, don't get into big trouble!"

Of course, I kept a mortified silence. The only words I knew to describe sexual parts were suitable for toilet training a two year old. I had absolutely no idea how to say birth control, and I wondered if *kondomu* would have anything near the correct meaning in Japanese. The passionate groans grew louder and more frequent. I swallowed hurriedly and retreated to the bathroom for a long and noisy shower. When I returned, the room was absolutely quiet. I turned down the light, got into bed and lay on my side. I smiled as I whispered toward you over in the Baby House, "Don't worry, baby, I will come and see you tomorrow."

Decide for the Wavering. When my husband and I returned the next week, we went to the Baby House to see you again. You had grown in just seven days. Your skin was now translucent and glowed like the moon through lotus petals. Your lips were pink as peonies and your nostrils were shaped like tiny hearts. I was surprised at how delighted my heart was to see you. I had been talking to you all week. "Don't cry, baby, we'll come to see you again soon." My husband carried you and smiled happily as you snuggled in toward him. I carried you and he took pictures. We put you down again on your side and then walked outside the Baby House and strolled around the orphanage grounds. "What do you think?" I asked. I felt as though we were walking along the shore of a deep, wide river; my doubts broke the surface here and there and glittered in the sun.

We walked in silence for a long time. We were two people in our forties, who through the years had developed the ability to be content whether we were together or apart. We walked past the August sunflowers blooming in the garden, past the shed in which the orphanage kept a small pony for the children to tend. Finally, my husband said, "She's a strong, perfect infant. We should adopt her. We will never get a chance like this again." I nodded my agreement, and together, we dove in.

In preparation for your plane trip home, Mrs. Nakasone showed us how to bathe you in the sink, and she dried you in a fluffy white towel. She then dressed you in the 100% cotton clothes we had brought and put you in our arms. "Feed her one bottle while the plane is about to take off, " she instructed. "The sucking motion will clear her ears. Burp her, change her, and then let her sleep. Feed her another bottle when the plane is about to land. This will clear her ears again." We repeated her instructions, wondering if we could remember enough to get you home safely.

Ignore the Ignorant. On our way back to Tokyo, we waited for our plane at the Kumamoto Airport. As we walked through the lobby, we became a team. My husband carried your many baby bags and I cradled you close. A middle-aged Japanese woman dressed fashionably in the light-colored silk suit, light stockings, and white shoes that were proper for August began following us and staring at you intently. We stopped while she peered into your face expecting her to compliment us on our beautiful child. Instead she scowled and scolded, "Isn't that baby not yet one month old? Why did you bring it out of the house?" Our Japanese is English accented and neither of us thought we had enough vocabulary to explain the intricacies of international adoption, so the only option we had was to walk quickly away toward our gate. We left the woman wondering loudly to anyone who would listen about the intelligence of people who would take an infant not yet a month old aboard a plane.

Live for the Dead. We forgot about her quickly. In the plane, we watched your face intently. We mixed the boiled water Mrs. Nakasone had packed at the orphanage with the powdered baby formula, shaking the bottle. We watched your eyes and your lips carefully. We were proud that you could suckle so strongly and proud that the pressurization of the cabin did not bother you. We pushed up the armrest between our seats and changed your diaper quickly. We took turns burping you and were proud that you could burp with authority. We watched every smile you attempted; we admired how calmly you slept. We never took our eyes off your face because those were the minutes in which we became your mother and father and you became our future. This was when we began doing what we will do for the rest of our lives, watching your face for signs.

Mavis Hara was born in Honolulu. She has a bachelor's degree from the University of Hawai'i and a master's degree from the University of California at Santa Barbara. She has lived in Hawai'i, Ohio, California, Alabama, Illinois, and Japan. She has been a military wife, a cancer survivor, and an adoptive mother.